Serafin

Another StarMaker Book by Sophie Masson:
The First Day

Other StarMaker Books:
Pagan's Crusade by Catherine Jinks
Neighbors and Traitors by Carole Duncan Buckman

Serafin

by Sophie Masson

ST★R_Maker_ **BOOKS**

Saint Mary's Press
Christian Brothers Publications
Winona, Minnesota

Jfic
Fantasy

To Camille, who loves the stories too.

Genuine recycled paper with 10% post-consumer waste.
Printed with soy-based ink.

The publishing team included Stephan Nagel, development editor; Laurie
A. Berg, copy editor; Alan S. Hanson, production editor and typesetter;
XXX, cover artist; pre-press, printing, and binding by the graphics division
of Saint Mary's Press.

Printed in the United States of America

Printing: 9 8 7 6 5 4 3 2 1

Year: 2008 07 06 05 04 03 02 01 00

ISBN 0-88489-567-X

10/00 *eng* 3.22

Author: Masson, Sophie
    Title: Serafin
Subject: 1. Young Adult—Fiction.
        2. Fantasy—Fiction.
        3. Spirituality—Fiction.
        4. Bible—Fiction.

Part One

Matagot

In those days as well as later, when the sons of the gods had intercourse with the daughters of mortals and children were born to them, the Nephilim were on the earth; they were the heroes of old, people of renown (Genesis 6:4, Revised English Bible).

» One «

There was nowhere to hide, nowhere to go. She could only stand and face them. Slowly, almost silently, the mob advanced. Catou could see the faces as they drew closer and closer: faces of people she had known from the first time she had opened her eyes on the world. There was Mamou the midwife, who had refused to attend her birth; there was Tonno the tailor, who thought himself so fine; over there was the miller, Sainton, and his two older sons, Gaspard and Gautier, mean-mouthed villains if ever there were any. No mercy to be expected there. She was a girl thin as a whippet, nervously bright as a snake, who had bitten them more than once after their clumsy advances. None there to help her, none. She clenched her fists and looked at them all, her black eyes with their strange yellow flecks bright with contempt. Fear beat inside her brain, but she would never think of retreating. She was the daughter of Mère Francou.

"Witch!" Gaspard cried, filling his mouth with the word as if it were some delicious sweetmeat. She turned her eyes on him, and for a moment he fell back, but then he was nudged by his brother, sly Gautier, and bellowed with more conviction, "Witch!"

"What would you people know of witchcraft?" Catou said suddenly, her voice clear and cold. "What would you know of anything beyond your little walls?"

They hated her, she knew that. She could see it in their dilated eyes, their twisted faces. They hated her because they did not understand her. With her black eyes, her dark skin, her hair almost the color of snow, she was a strange, arresting figure. She did not look like any of them here, but then neither had her mother, Mère Francou, who had turned up one day, heavily pregnant, and ensconced herself in a hut at the edge of the wood.

Some said Francou had come from the east, from beyond the rising sun. Certainly she had been utterly unlike anyone they had ever met before. She seemed to burn with an interior fire. Her eyes flamed into men's souls and did not flinch at what they saw. The villagers had not liked Mère Francou, but they had been afraid of her while she was still alive. Now she was dead and the daughter was alone, and they were not afraid of her—they had seen her growing up before their eyes. But they knew she was a bad thing, too unlike them, someone who shamed the village and must be destroyed.

Catou smiled. Her smile seemed terrible to them, for what did she have to smile about? Why was she not shaking, afraid?

"Do you know what you are doing?" she said clearly. "Be careful. Examine your hearts."

A voice at the back, a voice she did not for the moment recognize, called out: "Don't listen to her, good people. She is a mistress of lies and sorcery."

Catou looked for the owner of the voice but could not see him. It did not sound like someone from the village, though the villagers seemed not to care. They listen to strangers and want to destroy their own, she thought bitterly, but remembered what her mother had told her: "Never will you be of this place, my daughter," she had said. "Never, for you have been set apart. Your destiny is not here." When Catou was younger, she had not wanted to listen. She told her mother that she had played with the villagers' children, helped to heal their animals with her warm touch, that they liked her, trusted her, understood.

"I saw you but three nights ago, creeping in accursed *matagot* shape from your house." That was Tonno, pompous, fat Tonno with his unsuitably fine clothes. A *matagot!* That was their name for a cat-magician, a bringer of wealth but also a dark spirit that always exacted a price. *Matagot!* If they only knew. . . .

"Yes, I went out in my *matagot* shape, in my new fine red boots," she said. She crossed her arms and laughed. "Fine red boots, Tonno, and lace collar."

The crowd gasped. She was admitting it! And everyone knew what that meant. "We have wasted enough time." That voice again. "Why do we stand here gossiping like hens?"

"True enough." Gaspard was advancing toward her, his hands clenched on a length of rope. Catou stood her ground, back straight, heart beating wildly. Her mother's image flashed into her mind. Why had she been born, if it was to end like this?

"What are you doing? Are you out of your mind?"

A young man, little more than a boy really, had come panting through the crowd, red-faced, as if he'd been running. "Have you all gone mad? This is Catou. We've known her since she was born."

Frederic, the miller's youngest son, was a nice enough boy, but not very bright. As these thoughts flashed through Catou's mind, she was ashamed of them. Frederic reached his brother and laid a hand on his arm. "Gaspard, you must not do this. You will open us to the vengeance of the skies if you do this."

His brother pushed at him. "Don't be so stupid. What do you know? She is a witch. It has been proven. Why, she damned herself with her own mouth." Frederic glanced quickly at Catou, then away again just as quickly.

"You know the Law, my son. The Law we all live by." The miller spoke harshly. "Witches must die. So stand aside."

"No." Frederic moved directly in front of Catou. "I do know the Law. If there is one to speak for her, judgment may not be passed."

"Careful, Frederic," said his father, "you do not know all the Law."

"I know enough of it," his son said defiantly. From where she stood, Catou could see his Adam's apple bobbing convulsively. He is only a boy, she thought. How can he save me?

"So you are the one to speak for her?" Pompous Tonno asked again.

Frederic swallowed. "Yes, if no one else will."

He did not look at her. Catou thought that he did not really like her any more than the others. Although he had never been unkind to her, he had hardly seemed to notice her existence. So why did he . . . ? She shrugged inwardly. Living with her mother, she had learned not to ask too many questions. These people lived by the Law, their Law that was also hers, though they understood only a fraction of it. So much was hidden from them, more than they could ever dream of. And the fraction they knew spoke only of a harsh justice, a fear of strangers, of the unknown.

"So, speak for her." The voice at the back, amused now, as if knowing in advance what Frederic would say. Although Catou still could not see the man who spoke, there was something about his voice that she half-recognized with a wild beating of the heart, but could not quite place just yet. Her mother had said, "You will know your adversary when the time comes." But those had been words, just words, to a young girl who did not want to know she was different from the others. Now, of course, she *knew*. They had made quite sure of that.

"I speak for her because she is young. We have known her since she was a baby. We knew her mother. I cannot bring myself to believe she is a witch."

There was silence when he ended. Then Sainton spoke again. "If no one else speaks for her, if there is only one voice raised for her, it does indeed mean she escapes death. But she does not escape banishment. Nor does the one who speaks for her, if there is only one voice." He paused. "If there are any other voices to be raised, raise them now." No one spoke. Catou saw Frederic turn his head this way and that, something like fear dawning in his eyes. Poor fool! she thought. He'll change his tune soon. But he said nothing.

"No other voices." Sainton's eyes rested on his son without any indulgence. "That means banishment. For you, Catou. For you, my son. Catou is to be your only inheritance. Go, and take her with you."

Then Frederic's tongue was loosened. "But, Father! You cannot mean that!"

11

"It is the Law," Tonno intoned solemnly, before Sainton had a chance to open his mouth. Frederic tried again. "But that is unjust! That cannot be all of the Law! That is, is . . ."

But nobody answered him. Nobody looked at him. After a moment he understood that no one would speak for him. Slowly the crowd parted to let him—let them—through. Catou was the first to go, her quick steps taking her away swiftly. Frederic followed her more slowly, turning often, as if unwilling to believe what had just happened to him.

» Two «

He caught up with her at the end of the village. He did not look at her, and she did not try to make him do so, for she knew he would be weeping, and that would be as difficult for her as for him. She did not want to feel the painful tenderness she held in her heart just now. She had never experienced anything like it in her life before. Everything, to her, had always been so crystal clear, and now she truly did not know what to do, what would happen next. And she could not explain Frederic's actions. Some part of her, deep down, even scoffed at him for being ignorant of the consequences of that limited part of the Law his people knew. But still . . . still there was that tenderness, and she did not quite know what to do about it. At last, brusquely, she said: "You don't need to look quite so glum. We will not starve. I will see to that."

He shot her a quick look but did not speak. His eyes were indeed suspiciously bright, and she felt a sharp impatience rising in her. "You will find that I'm not such a poor inheritance as I seem to be."

Still he said nothing, so she continued, pride rising in her voice. "I will see that you are safe, then you will be rid of me."

This time, there was fear in his eyes, but still he said no word. *Dio,* but he was dense! If this was what it meant to be good, she did not know if she could understand it. With ordinary men such as his brother Gaspard, you always knew where you were; you could hit where it hurt. More to amuse herself than anything else, she said lightly: "With my help you can go any-where you want, be whomever you want to be. Why, we may go to the court of the King himself!"

"The King?" The simpleton had a look of such awestruck horror that she laughed out loud. "You cannot say such things. We are only villagers, and . . ."

"*You* may be," she pointed out, "but I was never so." Their eyes met, and she read in his a despair that made the tenderness inside her spread still further. "I was never allowed to be," she conceded, hoping to reassure him, hoping that the fierce shadow of her mother was not going to haunt her for this falsehood. For truth to tell, she and her mother had given the villagers as good as they had got. "Never forget," her mother had said. "Never forget you are not like these. Never!"

"No," he said, looking a little less like the sky had fallen on his head. Then he sighed. "But I do not understand what we are going to . . ."

"Don't concern yourself." Catou smiled. "You will see. Simply take what is offered. It is I who will concern myself with the details." She spoke more confidently than she felt, for although she understood a little of her powers, she did not know quite how far they would go. She did not want to let Frederic see even a quarter of them, and let's hope the poor fool doesn't take fright even at that. Then she thought of the voice in the village, egging the mob on, and she shivered, for she knew that soon she would be facing her true destiny, the one her mother had tried to make her understand.

» » « «

They walked for an hour or so, their feet getting sore in their heavy clogs, before coming to the local market town, Amadou. It was market day, and the roads were jammed with traffic. Frederic, who had not been to the town very often, wandered among the throng with a moonstruck expression. Catou kept herself separate from the crowds, but her eyes wide open for the first opportunity. They walked between stalls where people were selling wheels of cheese, high loaves of fresh bread, and live poultry. There were tables covered in bolts of fine and coarse cloth and a peddler with a tray slung around his neck, full of sweetmeats of all kinds. There were pens of pigs, young cattle

14

and rabbits, and fish slung on long sticks, gaping mouths survey-ing the sky. Catou's eyes narrowed when she saw them.

"You, Frederic, stay here. I will be back."

He nodded, his eyes and ears and heart too full of what he was seeing to move. He saw her slip off among the crowd but did not try to follow her. Really, he was a little afraid of her, which was strange because he had known her almost since the day he had first opened his eyes on the world, and especially be-cause in saving her, he had exiled himself. He did not want to think of that. He would concentrate on the future that might be opening to him. Strangely enough, he believed what she had told him. Frederic had always been scoffed at by his father and broth-ers for his trusting nature. And he always tried to believe the best of others; he could not keep gloomy thoughts in his mind for long.

"A beautiful sight indeed." The voice spoke at his elbow, and Frederic almost jumped out of his skin: *"Beau, mon ami, beau."* He turned to face his interlocutor, and saw a tall man in a plain suit of good cloth. His hair was long, as was the fashion, but plainly set and of a deep blond color. He had what appeared to be a natural beauty spot by the side of his wide, curving mouth, and a curling moustache. But it was his eyes that drew Frederic's attention: small eyes, of an unusual brightness, that appeared to miss nothing yet reveal nothing. The man looked prosperous—not one of your fops, but someone of real substance. Frederic smiled back.

"Yes, Sir. It is indeed."

"You are new to this town?"

"Oh, not exactly, Seigneur. I am from a village an hour's walk hence. But I have been to the town only two or three times in my life. It was mostly my brothers or my father who went."

"Ah." The stranger nodded. "It is exciting then."

"Oh yes, Seigneur. So many people!"

The stranger smiled. "Please, please, I am no seigneur. I am a simple man, my son. But where I come from, such crowds are nothing. I find it refreshing to be here."

Frederic looked at the man in some awe. "You are from a great city?"

"That is so. The greatest of them all."

"Oh," breathed Frederic, thinking of the greatest of them all, the huge city of Paris, and near it the King's palace. What his village had heard of such places defied description. For the first time, he thought that perhaps the rash words spoken by Catou —that they would go to the very court of the King—were true, that they might become true.

The stranger regarded him with good humor. "Perhaps I could take you there? It would be a pleasure to guide such as yourself to . . ."

"Oh no, Sir," Frederic burst out, rather discomfited by the suddenness of the invitation. "I am waiting for my friend, and I cannot go without her. We are going to . . ."

The stranger's expression did not change. "Of course, of course," he said politely, but Frederic had the distinct impression he was being laughed at. He began, uncomfortably, "Perhaps when she . . ." but the stranger had gone, quite vanished into the crowd. Ah well, thought Frederic as he turned back to surveying the scene around him with a slightly jaded eye, that is the way of the world. Strangers talk to you in crowds, then they disappear. And he felt pleased with himself for deducing this much already, despite a certain discomfort that remained with him.

And there was Catou, winding her way through the crowd. Over her arm she had a basket. "Let's get away from this crush," she said.

"This is nothing," said Frederic grandly. "In the city of Paris, there are such crowds as to make this merely a pleasant, quiet street."

Catou looked sideways at him. "And what would you know of that?" she inquired rather unpleasantly. It had been hard work getting the fish, and she was hungry and tired and in no mood for inanity. The man had almost got hold of her, but she had wriggled out of his hands and vanished with her prey. That had seldom happened to her before, and had made her think that she was allowing emotion to cloud her judgment. Maybe she had been more affected by the villagers' hate than she cared to acknowledge. She did not wait for him to answer her question, and did not notice his resentful glance. "We must get to somewhere quieter so we can eat."

Frederic wanted to argue, but his empty stomach suddenly made its presence felt. I won't tell her about the stranger, anyway, he thought resentfully. It would be his secret. When she annoyed him with her lordly ways, he would remember that he could have gone, could have planted her there, that he didn't really need her. But for the moment he was hungry. So he followed her with bad grace out of the busy square and toward the edge of the town, near fields that stretched in all directions.

Catou opened the basket. "Smoked fish," she said, handing him two damp parcels. "Fruit. Bread," handing him two dry ones. "And new shoes for us both." She spread them out on the grass: a new pair of serviceable, even smart, dark leather shoes with large buckles for him, a smaller pair of—and here he looked at her sharply, all his old fears returning—wine-red boots for her. She saw him looking at them, and smiled, the smile crinkling the corners of her eyes so that for an instant she did not look quite human, but more like a . . . a *matagot*. Hastily he pushed away the thought. He would not ask her any questions. He did not want to know the answers. She had obviously got all these things by some means it would not do to inquire about too closely. Besides, he was hungry. And she was right to get the shoes. They would have to walk leagues and leagues, and they could not do that in the broken-down clogs they had been wearing. He shrugged, and tried to look not only resigned but complacent. "Good. Let's be eating then," he said.

Catou, watching the emotions chasing themselves across his face, felt a hollowness inside her. She had not wanted him to ask questions, would have indeed slammed him sharply for them, so why did his reaction make her feel uncomfortable, almost fearful? That air of lordly unconcern on his face: if she knew it was a mask to conceal his real uncertainties, why did it disturb her so? She couldn't fathom it, and she was not used to lack of knowledge. Her separateness from the villagers had hurt, but the infernal pride it had engendered had always been a consolation. Were things changing?

» Three «

The sun was warm as they sat in the field eating, and their feet looked fine in the unaccustomed splendor of new leather. Frederic was excited and talked happily, while Catou nodded and listened. Catou watched her companion, her savior, her burden, and thought that really he was a very pretty boy, with his fine skin, easy blushes, and rich dark hair. My word, he would pass for a lord if his clothes were as fine as his new shoes. As fine a lord as any that passed in his carriage. She smiled, knowing that her fanciful ideas were close to the truth, for although there was much she did not know about her powers, she already understood much more than he. She knew, for instance, that the Law they all lived under had many degrees, and that most of the population would only ever understand a small fraction. She knew that some things were outside the Law. She knew that she herself was a part of its workings, in a mysterious manner. But she still did not fully understand or know what exactly her destiny would be. She was bound in a way Frederic and the villagers would never be, yet she possessed a freedom they could only guess at.

She did not see the glances he shot her as she sat eating her food, did not know the new notions that fizzed in his heart and his mind. Somehow the chance encounter with the stranger had opened his eyes to more than crowds. It had opened his eyes to possibilities, to ideas that would once have been as remote as the idea of leaving the village. Going to Paris, to the Court, even to see the King, no longer seemed totally outlandish. He spoke bravely and wildly of all they would do, not caring about her raised eyebrows, for freedom was opening to him too, a freedom he was still wary of but was slowly beginning to savor.

When they had finished, Catou jumped to her feet. "We have a long way to travel if we are to reach Paris before the next century."

At her words Frederic felt a tremor. "But it is a long way. Anything could happen on the way."

"Anything at all," Catou declared. "You are no longer of the village, my fine miller's son. When we left that place, everything you had once been became more. For you chose me as your inheritance, not your old ways, your family, your familiar skies."

The words were too cruel, too final: she saw that at once. She must remember that for him things were different, that he must have already been regretting his defense of her. She smiled. "Don't look so downcast. You will find that things outside the village are quite to your liking. And you will find that I know how to repay my debts. I have already started to do that. And I will not rest until I have paid fully: a life for a life."

He looked at her and saw that she spoke the truth. He had already seen how she could get them food, and these new shoes. But that was something that any skilled thief might do, was it not? Still, he had no option but to trust her, to allow her to do things for him, because it was obvious that somehow she had a knowledge of the world that he did not have. He was not ready yet to forgo that, despite the seed of ambition the stranger had planted. He shrugged, rather sulkily. "What I would like is not to walk. I have never much liked walking."

Catou said nothing for a moment, then in a tight voice: "There are some things you must do for yourself. Nothing is easily gained. There is a price for everything, Frederic."

But he looked at her challengingly, and she knew what he was thinking: if there is a price, it is you who must pay it, for I have paid already by forfeiting my old life. It was only to be expected, she thought, for he was a simple man, more like a child really—easily led, easily satisfied, yet with a certain sly tenacity about getting his own way. Perhaps it had been only squeamishness that had made him save her. But no, she must not count the debt, feel its weight. It was hers, and she must pay it. He had a chance to recant, and had not. She sighed. "But it is true, we cannot wear out our new shoes so soon. Wait here for me. I will return."

Of course she would return. How could a woman travel by herself on the roads? She needed him as much as he needed her, he thought. He smiled craftily. "I will wait."

Irritation crawled along her scalp as she left him. How long would she have to stay with this fool who was already treating her as if she had no option but to be attached to him? I could leave him, she thought. I have already done enough for him. But she knew she could not. It was her fate to be his inheritance, and she had to fulfill it to the last letter of the Law.

» » « «

Frederic lay on the grass in a blissfully unaccustomed idleness. In the village he would not have escaped the harsh eye of his father, would have been humping bags of grain and flour, killing rats, doing all the donkey work his brothers never did, simply because they were in his father's confidence. They were left the softer work of calling in debts, paying the Seigneur his bags of flour, and paying off various officials. Sainton's mill was run no more crookedly than any of the others in the district, but because he was an unimaginative, unbending man, it made less money than many. Before that day Frederic had never questioned his place in life, although he had often wept for his mother, whom he remembered as slightly more tender than his father. And he had always had time for surveying the small things his family passed by: the blue of the sky, the taste of the first fruit on the bough. His father thought him soft in the head, as did most of the other villagers. Even Catou thought that: he knew it from the look in her eyes. Lying there in the grass in the silent languor of a summer market day, when everyone was in town rather than in the fields, he almost wept, and was not sure why. He was set on his road now, and he had to take what came. But then he remembered the stranger and the way his eyes had lit up when

21

he mentioned the greatest city of them all. Frederic would go there too; he would become someone to be reckoned with.

He must have fallen asleep, for he did not hear her come back, just woke with a jump when a monster breathed into his face. Scrambling to his feet with a shout, he saw that the "monster" was in fact a rather sad-looking old nag, led by Catou. His embarrassment at being caught thus made him angry. "*That* is what is going to save our feet?"

Catou regarded him with disdain, and he flushed. He had never owned a four-legged conveyance of his own, not even an old nag like this. "It does not look as if it could go to the next village," he muttered, trying to look knowledgeable.

Catou shrugged. "If you do not wish to ride, you may walk."

"I did not say I would not ride . . ." But he was interrupted when she, with a swift, lithe movement, jumped onto the horse's back.

"Are you coming or not?" She held out a hand to him, which he took with reluctance, and clumsily tried to get up onto the animal's back behind her. The horse shifted and snorted, and Catou laughed as he struggled to right himself. Finally he was on. It did not feel good up there on the animal's bony back, but Catou touched the horse's neck gently, speaking in a voice so soft he could not understand her, and to his surprise it started trotting smoothly. It was alarming, for he had ridden on a donkey only twice, and on a horse never. The ground looked far away, and the unpredictability of animal creation suddenly struck him with force. He remembered an accident that had happened once on the road near the village: a horse had bolted, dragging its rider after it. When they had found the man, he had been barely recognizable. Frederic shivered, and all at once hoped fervently that the horse would *not* go further than the next village so that he would have an excuse to get off, and back onto firm ground.

» Four «

Catou seemed to have no such qualms. She handled the horse as if she had been born to it, though Frederic did not remember ever having seen her ride. It added to his growing catalog of uneasiness. But there was no question as to the girl's competence, and fortunately, Frederic's naturally kind and optimistic nature went with an indolence for which his father had often beaten him. He simply pushed unquiet questions to the back of his mind, and concentrated on present sensations.

Just once, Catou turned her head toward him, and he saw that her eyes were dancing with laughter. He straightened his back and pursed his lips, trying to convey his ease at being up there, jolted around like a poor sack of barley. Otherwise she trotted steadily on, talking occasionally to the horse, and after a while he forgot to be uneasy and started looking around at the countryside they were traversing.

There were people working in the fields, and some light traffic on the road, and here and there scattered houses. It was different country to his own: greener, with a richer look to it, a fatter look, somehow. He thought, yes, this is the kind of country I want, and as they passed by a large farmhouse, his heart filled with the notion that maybe one day he'd have something like this: a house with a clean floor and more than one pot to put on the fire, where sausages hung from the rafters and there were fat, yellow-fleshed chickens in the yard. And maybe a girl, a young woman, to share it with, though not one as thin and big-eyed as Catou, with her strange hair. She would be soft and round as a plum. And there would be children—many small, round children with hair the color of chestnuts. And he'd have a horse in the stable, and a painted cart, and a bright suit to wear on Sundays. His wife would have a green velvet ribbon to tie up her hair, and on special occasions they would take a basket of brown eggs and go in the painted cart to visit his father and brothers who'd be jealous, so jealous! Frederic smiled inwardly at the thought of Gaspard, his jutting jaw dropping in amazement when he saw his brother's prosperity. And in the fields he'd grow barley and rye and wheat, and his wheat would be the best in the district, so the finest flour would be made from it— flour so fine and white that the King's bread would be made of it. At the picture, Frederic was unable to resist a small squeal of pleasure, which caused the horse to start and Catou to frown. He frowned too, to show his impatience with the bag of bones they were riding on.

"When will we stop?" he asked, sulkily.

"When I come to the right place." Catou did not turn her head to speak to him, and Frederic felt aggrieved. He made a face at her back, which helped somewhat, then thought of how his father had called her his inheritance, and groaned to himself. It seemed he had merely gone from the harsh rule of his father to the disconcerting one of this odd girl. But it never occurred to him to abandon her. He was bound to her, he knew that much, because he had saved her. That was the Law.

Bound was how Catou would have described it too. She knew that until a certain time had arrived, she could not leave the young man. But she could have had a worse binding. At least his was a good nature, if he wasn't particularly bright. She was bound to go to the very end, though of what the end would be she had only a hazy notion.

They passed quietly through hamlets and small villages. A few people turned to stare at them, for it was unusual to see a woman riding a horse and a man behind, but they were not sufficiently unusual to draw the attention of the armed men, soldiers from the nobles' private armies, whom they saw occasionally. In this province, far from Paris but still subject to the radiating rule of the King, the nobles lived very much as they had lived for centuries, and their quarrels and friendships did not concern ordinary people very much, as long as the people's land was not in the way of some family dispute. The thing that most stirred country people against the nobles was their right to ride roughshod over land when they were hunting. Whole crops had been lost to the thundering hooves of noble mounts. In general, though, the nobles' armies kept to themselves, and it was rare indeed to see an official of the King. That would change as they pressed further north. In a few days they would be within sight of the King's seat of power. It would be like traveling to the center of the sun, and they would have to be careful not to get burnt.

Catou remembered conversations with her mother, Francou, lasting deep into the night, as Francou tried to teach her about the world and what she might find there. In her mind's eye, she could see her mother sitting by the fire, her eyes on the red embers, as if she could see past them into some other world.

My daughter, being in this small village is only a short rest along the road to your destiny, which lies beyond. It is not the whole world; it is not your whole destiny. She had turned to Catou then, her eyes, so similar to Catou's own, fixed on her daughter's face. *Your fate is mine, is more than mine. It is an ancient fate, an ancient calling, and we cannot escape it. There are not many of us left, but under the Law we must each accomplish our fate. The time will come—not so very far from now—when I will not be able to protect you any longer, so you must know these things. I cannot tell you fully, for it is hidden from me, but I can tell you that you will be bound under the Law, that you will face many dangers.*

But what dangers? What is the good of riddles? Catou had not wanted to shout, for her mother was already ill with the sickness that would eventually take her life. But she could not help it. She had not asked to have any fate other than an ordinary one.

Her mother had shaken her head, rather sadly, but with shining eyes. *I cannot tell you. For each of us, it is different. When the time comes, you will know.* And she had told Catou of a man she would meet, in a town to which she would journey, who would guide her further along her road. Then she had touched her daughter, held her, and Catou had smelled the death-smell on her, and her heart had been gripped by ice. *I will be watching,* her mother had whispered, *even though I will not be able to talk to you anymore. You and I, my daughter, our fate is one of power, of strength, but of a deep heartbreak too, of a pain not known to those outside us. We are in the Law, Catou. We are part of it. Yet it has bound us more than any of those ignorant creatures out there, because our nature is divided . . .*

These and many things Catou held in the most secret parts of her heart, parts that never saw daylight, had never been caught in words. Indeed, her mother had locked them there and enjoined her not to bring them out until it was necessary. She heard Frederic sigh behind her, and smiled to herself. How pleasing it must be to be born without knowledge, to live as if each new event were a complete surprise! The coldness of her own knowledge, even though it was incomplete, even though much was hidden from her—perhaps that was what had caused the villagers to turn against her. They felt instinctively that here was something unnatural. Only an innocent like Frederic, with his child's nature, was spared this recoil.

» » « «

Night was drawing in as they came into a small town. To Frederic's surprise, Catou drew up the horse outside a large, decorated inn with a neatly paved courtyard. Frederic knew they did not have the money to stay in such a place, and the disquiet leapt up in him again. But he followed Catou meekly enough, walking rather stiffly on account of his sore legs and buttocks.

"Are we sleeping in the stable?" he whispered as she led the horse up to the groom who was standing watching them at the door to the stable.

"Is that what you wish to do?" she asked.

"Isn't it what we must . . ." he began.

"Leave the obligations to me," she said, rather too sharply. Then she seemed to relent, and smiled. "Look." She reached into her pocket and pulled out a purse. She opened it. Inside were gold pieces. "See? We can pay."

Thunderstruck, he babbled: "But where did you? How did you?" But she put a finger to her lips, and he was quiet, though his heart still thudded. He followed her as she approached the groom, and his mouth was dry with fear and excitement.

The man stared curiously at their bedraggled appearance as they headed in the direction of the inn itself. As they walked, Catou said, her voice very low, very gentle, but somehow menacing, "In here you leave the talking to me. Understand?"

Frederic's heart was hammering in his chest, but he whispered, "Yes." What would she do? What would happen to them? He decided he didn't really want to think about it. He would simply take a deep breath, shut his mind, and do as she said. Absolutely. He had no choice. She could do anything: produce shoes, a horse, gold pieces out of the air. He did not want to know why or how. He would just follow.

» Five «

The inn was full of noise when they came in. The dining room was filled with travelers, and the girl who came to greet them was laughing merrily at some joke someone had made. She expressed no surprise at the sight of them, and showed them along dark corridors to a small but comfortable-looking room with two high beds, a table, a chair, and a basin of water. The floor was laid with old, round-cornered bricks and boasted a bright rug, and the linen on the beds looked fresh. As she left them, the girl said something that nearly caused Frederic to break his silence.

"When you and your companion are ready, Sir, we have some good dinner available."

"Thank you," said Catou, imperturbably, but when the door had shut on the other girl, Frederic turned on her.

"What did she mean, 'sir'?"

"People see what they want to see," said Catou, without a flicker of interest. She yawned, and Frederic knew that she would not say any more. But he had to.

"She called *you* sir! How can that be? You are a woman, that is plain to see. And me . . . well, I am no sir, and they would not put me in the same chamber as you if they thought you were a woman, and . . ."

"People see what they want to see," said Catou again. She stared at Frederic. "And I will not be sharing this chamber. I have work to do tonight."

A sudden shiver rippled over Frederic, and he said no more. Turning his back, he washed his face carefully, and his hands, all the while feeling the watchful yet detached presence of Catou at his back. But when he turned around again, she was not there.

She must have slipped out the door while his back was turned, though he had not heard the door opening or closing. He paused at the door, looking down the corridor, thinking she must have already gone in to dine. But she was nowhere to be seen. He stood there irresolutely for a moment, trying to still the unquiet thoughts that buzzed in his head. As he did so, a familiar voice hailed him.

"Well, if it isn't my friend who wants to see the great city!"

There was the well-dressed stranger he had met earlier. In the dimness of the corridor, the whites of his eyes shone like lamps.

"Oh, Sir, it is you!" Frederic laughed nervously.

"You are a long way from home now."

"My . . . my friend knows the way we are going, and . . ."

"Your friend, hmm?" The man came closer, and Frederic saw that his eyes were indeed shining, the dark of their irises glossy, lights dancing in them: whether of amusement or curiosity Frederic was not sure.

"Yes, my friend." Suddenly remembering what Catou had said about not speaking, he became confused, then irritated. Why should he wait for her? She was not here, in any case. He could not be expected to stay locked in the room while she roamed at her pleasure. He said firmly, "Yes, my friend, whom I was supposed to be dining with, but who appears to have changed opinion."

"Allow me to join you then," said the stranger, his smile never leaving his eyes. As they walked toward the dining room, he said, "Well, and how are you finding the road?"

"Tiring," Frederic said crossly. "We have an old horse whose ribs are like steel, and they bruise me so."

The stranger laughed. "I know the kind of horse you speak of! A farmer's horse." His bright eyes rested on Frederic, who flushed a little. "But you are bound for better things, are you not, my son?"

Frederic, suddenly suspicious, shrugged. "Perhaps. Perhaps not."

But the other man did not seem at all disconcerted.

Instead, he laughed again. "Spoken like a true son of the soil. Never giving anything away."

By now they had reached the door of the dining room. The room was not as full as it had been previously. Frederic saw at once that Catou was not there. But he was pulled along in the wake of the stranger, who conducted himself as if he were well known and respected here. Frederic thought suddenly that he still did not even know the stranger's name. Somehow there seemed no easy way to broach the subject. But then he was seated at the table, a plate brought to him, bread, a steaming meat dish, vegetables. His various uneases vanished as the smell of the food reached his nostrils, and his stomach rumbled in sympathy. He would find out all these mysteries later, he was sure of it. There was no need to be overly concerned. And, lulled by the food, the wine, and the stranger's friendliness, he spoke a little, and then a little more, and a little more. Catou was not there to frown, to chill, to stop a person from living as a person ought. So he ate and he drank and he talked, and the stranger listened and smiled and ate a little. And around them the life of the inn swirled.

All at once Frederic stopped talking. There was a quality to the stranger's listening that at last penetrated his sleepy mind. He grew sulky again, playing with the last bit of bread he literally could not fit into his mouth, and wondered where Catou was, and what she would say when she heard what he had been doing. All at once he looked up and saw an expression in the stranger's eyes that riveted him.

The man looked at him quietly for a moment, then he said, "Have you thought about what is in it for her? Why she is taking you like this? What she has in store for you?" Frederic was startled, for he had been careful not to refer to Catou as "she" out of some strange caution.

"I have wondered . . ." he said, reluctantly. "A sense of duty, I think. It is part of the Law perhaps?"

The stranger smiled, as if such a thing were a child's plaything. "Innocence is very sweet, but it will not save you," he said, very softly. "You should think carefully, my friend. I say this as a man of the world."

"But what can I do?" Frederic cried. "I am bound to her. I feel it."

"Bound? Bound? You should ask yourself how, why. And what is this Law you speak of? Is it the one all you people live under, or something more than that: dark, dangerous? Perhaps your villagers knew more than you."

Frederic stared at him, then away. "I cannot believe that."

"And perhaps you are right." The man's voice was smooth.

"In any case, we are going to the great city." A stubborn note entered Frederic's voice.

"In any case," the stranger agreed. His voice had an edge to it, his eyes an angry sparkle that Frederic did not notice. Frederic stared into his empty wine cup. "And then we will see," he murmured to himself. "We will see." He lifted his head. "Is that not the best . . . ?"

But the stranger had gone. He was alone at the table, the remains of his meal scattered around him.

But not for long, for in the next moment, Catou came into the room. He barely recognized her, for she wore men's clothes, her bright hair was pulled back, and on her head was a soft hat that she swept off when she reached his table. Only the boots were the same.

"I thought people only see what they expect," he said grumpily, all the while trying to still his thudding heart. Bound, he was. Yes, bound. But was it by some dark power, as the stranger had implied? And if that were so, what *did* she have in store for him? He thought of men who had lost their souls, and crossed himself furtively, carefully. But she appeared to take no notice. The sign did not seem to affect her in any way.

"I have new clothes for you, too," she said, ignoring his comment and throwing him a soft parcel. "You will be a new man."

"Thank you," was all he could think to say.

"You had a good meal?"

"Oh yes."

"And you did not speak to anyone?"

"No," he lied, sullenly. What right did she have to tell him what to do? Bound he might be, but surely not a slave.

"I think the innkeeper thinks we are spies for the King." Catou smiled suddenly. "That is why we are getting such good treatment. This town was the center of a rebellion some time ago, and now it is trying very hard to prove its loyalty."

"A rebellion?" Frederic seized the topic gratefully.

"A certain nobleman thought himself strong enough to challenge the King. He was not from here, but he found support here. The King's revenge was terrible."

"Oh." There was that in Catou's eyes that made him feel uncomfortable. "That is the way of all rebellion."

"Yes, when that rebellion is not for the good, but the bad. That nobleman was known as a wicked man. The things he had in store for the country would have caused rivers of tears to run."

"What happened to him?"

"He is in the Bastille. A living death. He cannot speak or see daylight. He is in eternal darkness. He cannot even see his own face, for they have covered it with a hideous mask of molten metal."

Frederic shuddered. "That is a terrible vengeance."

"But deserved, for he broke the law of the King." Her face was like a mask itself for a moment. Then it broke up as she smiled, more kindly this time. "Come and get changed, and rest. Tomorrow we have a long way to go."

At the door to the chamber, she paused. "There is something I must do tonight. Please do not try to follow me, or to question me. Sleep. That is what you need. I will be here in the morning. That is all you need to know." But he did not want to go back into that silent room where the doubts and questions and fears would plague him. He said, "Why can't you take me? I am strong, good with my hands. I could protect you. You are a weak woman, and the streets are not safe."

Her eyes flashed. "I am well able to take care of myself. I do not need you."

"Yes? What, then, of the village? You would have died there if not for me."

Silence. Then she said, much more gently, "I am sorry, Frederic. What you say is quite true. But please understand that you cannot come with me." She raised a hand as if to touch him, then let it drop again, as if she couldn't quite bring herself to do so.

"Well, then," he said, feeling a strange sadness at her reluctance, "I will not stay in my room like a prisoner. I will change, but I will then go to the taproom and be in company. I do not want to be on my own."

"As you wish."

The gentleness in her eyes had gone. Instead they condemned him for his inability to be solitary. But he would take no account of that. She could think whatever she liked. She had not said do not speak to anyone, for she had known that in such a place you could not fail to speak and be spoken to. Perhaps she had decided that he could not be stopped. Perhaps he had won a small victory.

» Six «

There was a merry party in full swing when Frederic pushed open the door to the taproom. He and his brothers had often spent a good hour or two or three in such company, so it was with a sweet sense of familiarity that he merged into the crowd. For a moment he thought of Catou, alone in the dark streets, but then he shrugged the thought aside. She had not wanted his company, that was plain. Frederic rarely wasted time in vain regrets or speculation. Now he allowed all his concerns to slip from him as he drank deeply of the good beer and wine on offer and made lighthearted·conversation with a girl who was as plump as she was pretty. He would not be lonely tonight.

» » « «

Towns were never as quiet at night as people imagined them to be, Catou thought as she prowled along the streets. Every sense was alert, every nerve strung. In the distance she could hear the trudge of the town watch, patrolling the streets in their often rather inefficient way. Closer by she could hear rustles: furtive movements that might have been rats or imprudent townspeople out late or malefactors of one sort or the other. The King's peace did not always reach down to towns like this, and even if it did, it was almost impossible to hold an entire populace within the Law. Someone always thought they could get away with flouting it, even though the punishments were so severe. Catou grinned ferociously to herself as she thought of what Frederic would do if he could see her now.

Her mother had told her that she must make this meeting when the time came for her to fulfill her destiny. Now she was in this town, in the very street her mother had told her about,

34

and her heart thudded with the realization that things were moving now, that soon she would know more.

She stopped at a door. It looked just like all the other doors in the narrow street, but she knew it was the one. Softly, she called. As she did so, she became aware of a slight movement in the shadows opposite. She stiffened, the hair on the back of her neck erect. Then she saw it was a rat, a rat that stood regarding her, its eyes bright as jet, its nose twitching. Catou's body stiffened, but at that moment the door opened and a voice said, "I've been expecting you." A smile, then the man said, "Come on, there's no time for rats," and she was ushered in, stepping delicately through the open doorway, her body still tingling from that unexpected encounter.

"Ah." She breathed deeply, stretched, relaxed again. This was the one, then, whom her mother had told her about. In the presence of one of her own kind, she could feel both less lonely and stronger. He watched her transformation and smiled again.

"You are weary. Sit down." It was not exactly kindness in his voice, but a recognition of fellowship. He brought a drink, a thick slice of bread, some meat. He watched while she ate and drank, then silently took the plate and cup away. Then he said, "You have come a long way, but there is still far to go."

"I know," she said, looking at him: into the eyes that were so like hers, the face whose age could not be pinpointed, the looseness in the limbs that spoke of a transforming power like her own.

"Your mother . . . I knew her, once." His eyes flickered a little. "It is a great sadness to know she has died. There are not many of us now. And we are not understood by those we are born to serve."

Catou refused to be drawn into sadness. She said, "My mother said you would know the next step, that you would tell me what must happen."

He nodded, rather wearily. "Yes. But you understand that the full picture is hidden from me, as it is from you. I know that it is your destiny to allow the young man you serve to reach his full being, that you are there not only to protect but also to transform his life. But there are two sides to our fate, as there are two sides to our nature. We must learn, too. We must learn to understand not only the Law but also our own divided selves. We must face the Adversary. And it is in our divided selves that true freedom from the binding will come, as will defeat of the Adversary, for there is no division in his nature, only a seeming subtlety. You will know what it is that can save you when the end is near, just as I did when my time drew near, even though my freedom is different from yours. Although we are of one kind, each of our unbindings is different."

"So you do not know what will happen to me?"

He spoke gently. "No. I cannot. Your power is similar to mine, yet different."

"But I cannot even fully understand it! I know I can transform my shape; I know I can perform simple acts of what people here call magic. And I can see the haziness of the future. But I cannot focus on it, I cannot! Why are we tortured so? If we are to be different from others, if we are messengers in part of our nature, why cannot we have full powers, full understanding?"

"Because our destiny lies in our divided nature. Because of what happened at the dawn of the ages. Because we are not of one or the other, yet of both."

Catou made an angry movement. Then, containing herself, she said, "So, what will happen? What is the next step?"

"You will come to an enchanted place," he said carefully, looking at her. "It is a place of shadows and of spells, but also a place of golden dreams. There your destiny will unfold: yours and that of your bondman. You must be careful, for this place is also that of the Adversary, and there will be attempts made to change you. You will need to be strong, for the Adversary works in many different ways, and he will speak through many mouths. He will be both servant and master; he will have a seeming humility and a hidden power. You will know him, for that is part of our memory, part of our ancestral nature, to recognize him. But first you will arrive at a river . . ."

He spoke for a long time, while she listened, taking careful note in her head, her heart. She spoke very little herself, except to clarify some points. When it was clear he had finished, she thanked him and sat silently for a moment.

"And you know no more, then?" she said, after a while. "You do not know what will happen at this enchanted place?" He shook his head. She sat quietly for a moment more, then lifting her head, she looked him full in the face, this young man with his old, old eyes, and said, "Didn't you ever rebel, in your heart, against our fate?"

He regarded her steadily, gently. Then he said: "Yes. But then I learned who I truly was: not only my fate, but about myself."

She nodded slowly, then stood up. "You have been very kind, despite my anger. I will remember all you have told me. I thank you."

"No thanks is due," the other said. "That is part of the Law. But . . ." and he hesitated, "I will give you this: just remember, do not discount the things you may think most humble. They may save you all in the end."

She looked at him quickly, then away. "I will try to remember."

"One more thing." He got up and left the room for a minute or so, then returned with something wrapped in parchment. "A gift for a king." He held it out to her. "You will know when to give this." Now he touched her, very briefly, on the shoulder, and she felt the touch thrill through her like a cold fire. He smiled, dazzlingly. "Good-bye, then. Good-bye." And her last sight was of him standing straight and tall in his simple room, the smile playing on his lips, the secrets they both shared shading his beautiful eyes.

» »   « «

In the taproom the noise was deafening. The room was full of people now, some shouting, some singing, others talking at the top of their voices. It was a cozy, convivial atmosphere, but for the last few minutes, Frederic had not felt at all well. His new friend had deserted him to go and sit on the lap of a fine gentleman in lace and satin, and the beer had gone not to his head but to the pit of his stomach, where it sat like dread. A fluttering kind of panic agitated in his throat. What was he doing here? Where was Catou? Where were they going next? What was going to happen to him? He looked at the faces around him, red with merriment and tipsy fellowship, and suddenly they looked leering and mocking to him. Frederic thought of the man who had spoken to him earlier, about his warnings, and shivered. Suddenly he got up, lurched away from the table, and out toward the door. No one noticed his departure; the crowd closed around his absence as if he had never been there in the first place.

Outside, the night was at least clear and cool. He shook his head like a dog, but that only sent dizziness spinning through his skull. The beer here in town must be far stronger than anything he had ever had in the village, where it was drunk not long after it was made and was light and refreshing. He didn't belong here in this place, and in Paris even less. Misery rose in him, making tears prick in his eyes. He just wanted to be like everyone else, he thought. He just wanted an ordinary life among his own people, not something risky and unknown. But now he could not go back to the village. He was forced to go where Catou wanted, for she knew things he could have no inkling of. As he stood there, he became aware of a presence next to him. Without turning, he knew it was the man who had spoken to him earlier.

"I agree. The fumes in there are enough to make a man sick."

The voice was light, amused, and for some reason, it both reassured and unsettled Frederic. He turned to face the man. "I think the beer is adulterated here. It makes me feel odd."

"Ah yes. That is quite possibly the case." The man nodded wisely. He paused, then, "Your friend is not with you?"

"No." Frederic did not want to talk about it. After a while, he added, with a determined effort, "And you, Sir, are you making a journey of pleasure or returning home?" He could not keep the longing from his voice when he said *home*. And yet home had rejected him.

"Oh, I do beg your pardon," the man said smilingly. "I have not even introduced myself." His eyes were fixed on Frederic as he spoke, and the young man had the unsettling thought that the stranger knew very well who *he* was. "My name is Balze," he went on. "I am in the service of a great lord, the Lord of Tenebran. I am on business for him and must return there tomorrow."

"Oh." Frederic stared at the man. He had heard of the Lord of Tenebran from his new friends in the taproom. He was a man of immense wealth, a recluse, but known as a tyrant. "He's a real ogre!" one of the girls had said, giggling in fright. "Anything is his, anything. He has power, money, everything; he takes just what he wants."

The man seemed to read Frederic's thoughts. "I see you have heard tales." He smiled at Frederic. "I do assure you, my dear friend, that tales grow in the telling. People are jealous, afraid of power yet greedy for it."

"His castle is near here?"

"About two days' travel from here. Not far from Paris itself. It is a most beautiful place, with everything the heart could desire: magnificent gardens, beautiful rooms, food and drink in plenty, plays, gracious living."

"Oh . . ." Frederic's eyes shone.

"Perhaps you will go there," the man went on. His eyes were very bright. "You can judge for yourself then."

"But Catou . . . But I . . ."

The man shrugged. "If you do go there, just remember I am there. I will help you in whatever way you need."

"*Help* me?" Frederic's gaze was troubled.

"You are in danger, my friend, even if you do not know it."

"Why should you want to . . ."

"Because I like your face. Because you look honest. Because I *can* help you." Smiling, he bent down and picked up a stone, which he threw expertly into the shadows opposite. There was a yowl, a skitter of paws, and a cat shot past them and around the corner. "Always disliked cats," he said, in answer to Frederic's mild astonishment. "Self-contained beasts." He turned to Frederic. "And now, my friend, I think I really must get to bed. My Lord of Tenebran will not be impressed if his servant is hollow-eyed and incapable. Good night. And remember, the way to Tenebran is open."

"Thank you. Good night." Frederic wanted to tell him to stay, but he felt a strange reluctance at the same time. He stood for a while after the man had gone, his confused thoughts tangling. Maybe it would not be so bad after all. Home was not the only place. Perhaps on the road ahead lay riches untold, dreams of love, ease such as he had never known.

Part Two

The Marquis

» Seven «

When Frederic went back into his room, he saw that the other bed was occupied. A shape was humped under the bedclothes. Clothes were folded neatly on the chair, the red boots standing stiff in the moonlight that slanted into the room as if they still held feet. "So she's back," he grumbled to himself. "About time."

He climbed into his own bed, clothes and all, and was almost instantly asleep.

When Frederic awoke, the bed opposite him was empty. He struggled upright, his head heavy, his tongue thick. Ugh, he thought. Never, never again. Bread and water for me from now on. Then he grinned. How many times had he made that kind of a vow?

He swung his legs out of bed and got up. He ran a hand through his hair, pulled at his rumpled clothes in a vain attempt to make them presentable, and put on his shoes over his wrinkled stockings. He splashed some water over his face. There, that would do. His chin felt bristly. He would have to find a barber soon, but for the present he needed a good, hot drink.

Catou was alone in the inn's dining room, elegant in her new men's clothes, eating steadily. When she saw Frederic at the door, she raised her eyebrows. "Good *morning*."

"It's still only early." Frederic flushed at the implied reproach.

"And we must be on our way." She waved a hand to a chair. "Sit down. Eat. If we are to reach our destination this week, we cannot waste any more time."

What time had they wasted? Frederic sat down sulkily.

"Here. This is good." She pushed a cup toward him.

Despite her casual words, there was something almost desperate in her eyes, so that his tender heart was touched. "Catou, you look so tired."

"I am," she snapped, turning her head away. "But no matter."

He drank in silence, dipping some bread into the milk too, and finding it good. His head began to clear, and he was starting to feel almost himself when she said, "Phew, you've slept in those clothes, have you not? You smell like you have been in a tavern brawl."

"And so?" He was unruffled. "Humans smell. That is our condition." But now that he came to think of it, there was no such smell coming from her, none of the aroma of hot, seldom-washed skin. She smelled cool, like the night.

"Where we are going, you will need to think differently."

"And where are we going? Still Paris?" He was stung by her tone, and looked at her challengingly.

She did not answer him directly. Instead, she got up and smoothed down her immaculate clothes. "Be ready very soon."

He said nothing, but chewed his bread with exaggerated emphasis. She stood there for a moment looking at him, then banged out of the room, and he could hear her in the corridors talking to someone, presumably the landlord.

Frederic sat in his seat, determined to enjoy his meal to the last, refusing to be hurried by anyone, let alone such a one. It wasn't natural, he thought sulkily, that a woman should be so. Now if she were his wife, things would be different. He would tell her what was what. But the thought of the spiky Catou being his wife was just too fantastical to entertain. Instead, he fell into daydreams of a sweet, tenderhearted woman with melting brown eyes and hair the color of chestnuts, round limbs as soft as dough, and a ready smile. That would be the sort of woman for him.

》 》 《 《

They had been riding in silence for quite a while, and had passed through several villages and hamlets. Traffic had increased noticeably, as had the number of people in the fields. Bustle everywhere. In one village a market was taking place as they rode through, and they stopped for a few minutes to buy some bread and a corner of cheese that they ate as they rode along. Toward midday, though, they took a road that skirted the bank of a river, and then at last they were stopping.

Once on the ground, Frederic rubbed at his legs and his bottom. "That horse is made of iron," he grumbled. "And it prickles."

"Have a swim then." Catou was rubbing down the horse, her hands busy over its hot flanks.

"A swim?" He glanced quickly at her. "But I . . ."

"Leave your clothes on the bank. They'll be quite safe. And don't worry, your modesty will be quite safe with me. I am not going to watch you. I have more important things to do."

Again he was stung. He'd been considered quite good looking in the village, and Catou's indifference was galling. Still, he was glad when she walked off, down around a bend in the river. He glanced around. No one else there. The horse, released from bridle and saddle, stood placidly munching the grass. The sun beat down, and the water looked so inviting, he could not resist. He slipped out of his clothes, put them carefully under a big rock, and jumped into the water.

He had learned to swim at home, after having been thrown into the river by Gaspard, who had thought it a huge joke to see his little brother floundering in the water. He had paddled energetically, his heart thumping, to the bank, but had so enjoyed the sensation that he had done it again and again. Frederic remembered the baffled look of fury on Gaspard's face when that had happened, and he laughed out loud now at the memory. Since that day, he had spent many happy hours in the river—a love that was not shared by many, as the river was considered dangerous. Now he turned on his back and watched the sky, flipped over and dived, felt the silky water rolling off his shoulders and his back and his legs, and was happy. That was one of his gifts— a capacity to be happy, in a moment, in a trice.

Catou, watching him unseen from a tree, felt the gentleness that had begun to cloud her vision when it came to Frederic. She noticed his careful positioning of his clothes and smiled to herself. She watched his practiced dive, his smooth swimming, his obvious enjoyment of the water with some envy. Then she stopped watching and listened carefully. Yes, she could just hear the sound she was expecting, in the distance. She jumped lightly down from the tree and padded off quickly in the direction of the sound. As she ran, her heart pounded with the thought that this was the turning point. This was the place of no return.

>> >> << <<

Frederic had splashed about happily for some time before feeling a little cold and climbing out onto the bank to dry off a little. It was wonderful to be alive, he thought, stretching, the breeze blowing gently on his bare skin. He would put his clothes back on and go and see if Catou was anywhere about. He walked over to the stone where he had put his clothes, only to discover to his horror that they were gone. In the same moment, he heard a rumble of wheels and saw, coming toward him rather fast on the riverside road, a very elegant carriage with someone leaning out of a window. Panic filled him, and without thinking, he sprang back into the water and crouched under it, with only his head visible. Hopefully the fine carriage would simply pass by. But, oh horror! It stopped right near him, and a voice he knew only too well, but filled with unaccustomed urgency, rang out. "Quick, yes, that's him. Oh, quick, quick! Oh, my poor master!"

Two burly men jumped off the carriage footplate and came splashing toward him. Frederic was far too amazed and terrified to do anything at all as they grabbed hold of his arms and pulled him bodily out of the water. One of the men held a large embroidered robe, which he put around Frederic as soon as they were on dry land. He said, "It's dangerous country, my Lord."

My *Lord?* Frederic was numb with fright, but managed a slight nod. Then Catou stepped down out of the carriage, followed at a short distance by a short, rather fat man in splendid clothes. The latter approached Frederic with a broad smile. "My dear Marquis!"

"My master, the Marquis of Carabas," said Catou in a warning tone of voice, "is still in shock from his dreadful experience."

"I am afraid," the short fat man said, "that we are not rid of malefactors yet."

Frederic, almost dead with fear, could manage to say nothing, but tried to smile. The short fat man did not appear to find this at all strange.

"My Lord, my master the Marquis was set upon by ruffians and his clothes stolen," said Catou in that new deferential but warning tone.

She was mad. Totally crazy. How could they hope to get away with this one? It had been one thing to charm people into giving them food and a horse and a bed at the inn, quite another to make up a whole new identity for him. Frederic felt desperately sick. "Ah . . ." he began, and then stopped as he saw another figure step down from the carriage. And from the moment he saw her, all thoughts of resistance fled.

She was not the dough-armed, melting-eyed image he had dreamed of, which now vanished, never to be seen again. She was small and slight as a bird, her carefully dressed hair black as a crow's wing, her eyes a startling vivid blue. She was dressed in pale satin and lace, and came stepping hesitantly toward them, her eyes on the group. As she came nearer, her eyes and Frederic's met, and in that instant he was in love. He saw that her eyes flickered too. And then she said, in a sweet, low voice, "Surely we should not stand here talking when the poor Marquis is obviously so distressed."

Frederic gulped. He would be anything, anyone, as long as he could be near her. If he had to be the Marquis, if that meant keeping quiet for a while and letting Catou do all the talking, so be it.

"My dear daughter." The short fat man patted the girl on the hand. "You are, of course, quite right." He turned back to Frederic. "Please, Sir, do us the honor of stepping into our carriage." He waited, beaming, while Catou "translated." "We have, alas, no extra clothes with us, but you will find that Tenebran is more than equipped with such things. I am sure my brother, the Lord of Tenebran, will concur with me when I say that you are welcome for as long as you wish to stay." He smiled at what he took to be Frederic's confusion after Catou again translated. "Your servant has told us the whole lamentable story: about your old family in Spain, your brothers' treachery, your flight to France with only your faithful manservant, and now your present sad plight. I have heard many tales of Spain, but I confess I have never been out of our own country, and indeed I can understand how grievous this must be to you. I know you do not understand much French as yet—how merciful that your servant is a native of this country—but I hope you understand that we are most honored to have such a distinguished guest."

This speech filled Frederic with an excitement and an admiring hilarity he found it difficult to keep from his features. His extraordinary good fortune was so overwhelming that he quite lost all his fear, even though he had heard the name *Tenebran* with some surprise and even disquiet. Without looking at Catou, who stood humbly to one side, he nodded his head, smiled, and said something in his own village patois, hoping both that the short fat man would not recognize it, and also that he wouldn't know that it wasn't Spanish. From the smile that spread over the man's kind, rather foolish face, Frederic guessed he was in luck. His head and his heart were light in a way that was quite like intoxication, but far sweeter. He saw the girl's intent eyes on him and suddenly walked over to her. He bowed low, and with a catch in his voice that was half-fear and half-thrill, said in patois, "Already, I cannot leave. . . . Already, I am bound to you." She did not understand the words, that was plain, but he was sure she understood their import, for she flushed with pleasure, and her father looked gratified.

"My Lord Marquis says he would be honored beyond words to come with you, and that he will remember this day and this riverbank as the sweetest of his life," Catou said, deadpan. All at once Frederic wanted to hug her. But of course he didn't. He merely nodded, rather regally, and followed the rest of the excited party back to the carriage. In his sweetest dreams he could never have hoped for this, but now he followed as if he were enchanted, as if every step he took were blessed. The fear and confusion of the last few days had vanished. It was almost as if he were entering a time, a space outside all boundaries, a state of enchantment beyond all dreams. For a moment he thought of Balze, the stranger in the town and at the inn. He was from Tenebran. He would know who the young man really was. But Frederic also knew, with a certainty born of enchantment, that none of it mattered. He was being borne along swiftly to his real home, his true destiny.

» Eight «

The carriage rattled swiftly along the riverbank road, the splendid horses trotting as if filled with the joy of being alive. Frederic's heart sang as he swayed to the motion of the carriage. He had exchanged few words with his hosts, and those in a halting way, as much from shyness as from the need to play the part. But the glances he had exchanged with the girl conveyed more than the finest plays of the most refined court writer. Catou was outside, sitting with the driver, and in this scented moving room, Frederic could truly, *had* truly, become the Marquis of Carabas. He saw that both the girl and the fat nobleman, her father, accepted him completely as one of their own. He did not question this miracle, for he knew miracles happened. Was it not a miracle that the sun rose every morning, and that God sent his own good rain in time for crops? And had God not shown him he must defend Catou, so that he could be rewarded in this way? For a second he thought of Catou, and the stranger's warnings and insinuations the other night, but the thought was not urgent. What did it matter? He was here, being borne swiftly to a wonderful destiny. He was in an enchantment from which he would never want to emerge.

Outside, Catou watched the countryside unfolding rapidly as the carriage swept through it. She saw how it changed from green and fertile to bare and bleak, how the shapes of the hills were barebacked, the ridges like deeply scored bones. They passed fields of stone and stunted grain, where peasants poorer than any she had ever seen toiled with bent backs, and where blank-faced children with features as deeply scored as the hills watched them pass by without a sound. Although the sun was still shining, somehow its brilliance here had become transmuted

49

into something harsh and deathly. A feeling of hopelessness filled her. They were not going to a good place, she thought. They were going to a dangerous place, to the place where everything would be decided. And her freedom, her own destiny, lay there, as much as did Frederic's.

The driver pointed a whip. "Look: Tenebran!" In the distance, rapidly approaching, roofs and turrets glittered in the sunshine. Nearer, and they resolved themselves into a series of square and round roofs and small turrets, most beautifully tiled in a blue-gray that shone like silk. Closer still, and she could see the infinitely shining thousand window-eyes of an elegant castle, a castle made of a soft pale stone and decorated with arches and curves. The ugly countryside was forgotten in the sheer beauty of the place. As the carriage rattled into the grounds of the castle, her heart rose. There were gardens laid out in intricate patterns around the main buildings, lakes and fountains, statues, and long walks of gravel where she could see figures moving. The sun played on the stone and the water and the green of the gardens, and made this a world of its own. She wondered what Frederic must be thinking as he looked out on all this magnificence. In heaven. He must think he has died and gone to heaven.

The carriage stopped. The footman ran to open the door. Catou stepped down too, while the driver stayed where he was, ready to take the entire conveyance to the stables. Out stepped the fat man, then the girl, helped down by her father, and last Frederic, still clutching the rich robe around him. Catou, watching him, saw the smile breaking over his face like the sun, and thought, yes, he is most uncommonly handsome. He had a natural grace and bearing with which she had not credited him. In this setting even the bristles on his cheek looked like a mark of nobility, a suffering nobility that would probably see him become the focus of all eyes. She hoped he would have the sense to keep quiet though. If he really opened his mouth and said what was in his kind but commonplace mind, he would be in the deepest trouble.

"Well." The fat man nodded. "Welcome to Tenebran." He called to some servants who had come hurrying out of the castle. "This is the Marquis of Carabas. He is to be looked after as if he were from Tenebran: new clothes, a bath, anything he may desire. The same for his servant. And a cold lunch for us all in my chambers."

Frederic inclined his head graciously and said, in patois, "Oh my God, I never thought to see such a place, not even in my dreams!"

Catou, face straight, translated: "The Marquis of Carabas thanks you infinitely, Your Lordship. Your kindness is greater than the sun."

A look of unease passed over the fat nobleman's face. "Quite so, quite so," he said hurriedly. "Come on, my dear, we must be ready too. And my brother will be waiting to hear the news from the north. We will see you very soon, my dear Marquis. I sincerely hope you will find Tenebran to your liking."

His daughter said nothing, but her blue eyes rested on Frederic in a way that even the hardest heart would have found affecting.

>> >> << <<

"Catou," Frederic said, when at last, bathed and dressed, they were by themselves. "Catou, I am afraid." He flung himself down in a chair and stared at his "servant." "Catou . . ."

"Don't be afraid," Catou snapped. "Just accept. You will be fine, as long as you do that." She prowled around the room. It was a smallish but splendid room, hung with tapestries and featuring a painted ceiling in the most modern manner, with cherubs and shepherdesses and much gilt. There were several chairs, an ornate writing table, and a bed so stiffly hung with silver brocade that it was difficult to imagine sleeping in it.

Just to one side was a narrow corridor that led to a much smaller room with a simple bed and chair. This was to be Catou's, a situation for which she was most grateful. As a servant, she had, strangely enough, more privacy than a noble, for nobles had servants dogging their footsteps. They could not take a bath without someone to hand them soap, towels, creams, clothes. They could not eat without a servant to give them plates, glasses, steaming dishes. They could not be on their own to think or weep or simply rest. And the higher the noble, the worse it was, so that at the very top, the Sun King himself was never without another human face at any second of his life. Even the most basic natural function of all had to be accomplished without privacy, and yet the humblest servant had his own time, alone at night.

Ah, you can keep your finery and your riches, Catou thought harshly as she watched Frederic. Your freedom is over, my lad. No more swimming in the river on your own, no more drinking in the tavern, no more thoughts of your own. This is another binding—a binding you take on gladly, but still a binding. And yet she knew that while she felt like that, Frederic did not. Even in the village, people did not like to be on their own. Wasn't that one of the reasons why she had been regarded with such suspicion—because she did not seem to be the same as they?

She thought about what the man had told her in the town—was it only last night?—and sighed inwardly. They were not done yet with bindings.

"My Lord Marquis," she began. Frederic interrupted her. "It feels strange to me, this name," he said. "It makes me feel odd, as if all my other life has disappeared."

"And so it has," said Catou. "You are now a new man. Look at yourself." She beckoned him to the huge gold-rimmed mirror in one corner of the room. "Come here and see."

Obediently, Frederic did so. He saw a tall, well-made young man with shining, dark brown hair brushed back into fashionable waves, a man whose long-lashed golden eyes made him look both unusual and handsome.

He was now dressed in the finest linen and cambric under breeches of a soft golden brown cloth and a coat of the same color, shot through with deep green. At his throat and sleeves, a cascade of lace; on his legs, deep-green stockings that showed off his calves and fine ankles, and on his feet, medium-heeled shoes of soft pale leather. Frederic gulped a little at his transformation, then smiled, almost involuntarily.

"Yes, see, you are very much the picture of the modern marquis," Catou said dryly.

He could see her in the mirror, dressed in the sober but good-quality clothes of a trusted personal servant, her strange hair powdered so as not to look as out of place as usual. He could hardly think of her as female anymore. In any case, she had never fit his notion of womanhood.

She saw his glance. "It may be better if you do not call me Catou any longer either," she said, and saw, with a slight tremor of hurt, the relief in his eyes, relief that he could forget the past. "You had better call me Serafin. That is a good name for such as I."

"Serafin. What a strange name," the Marquis of Carabas said idly, turning a little to catch sight of his back reflected in the mirror. "Well, if you think it's best. Now, do I recall there was talk of a cold lunch?"

The enchantment is complete, Catou thought. Here at least, in this place where destiny awaits, simple Frederic has truly become a great nobleman. She could see it in his eyes, and for a moment she was afraid, for the spell did not hold for her; she still saw the truth.

» Nine «

The Lord of Tenebran, he whose castle this was, did not attend at lunch, but his brother, Monsieur de Saint-Cotin, the Count who had brought them here, said they would meet him very soon. Monsieur's daughter, whose name was Elisabeth, they had discovered, told them in her sweet, gentle voice that the Lord of Tenebran was a most reclusive man and that he had his own way of doing things—a piece of noninformation that intensely irritated Serafin, as she now was, but charmed the Marquis. Little by little, it appeared, the magic of Mademoiselle Elisabeth's presence was working on the tongue of the Spanish Marquis. His French was growing by the minute; his voice more purely enunciating the words, though still with a quaint accent that betokened his foreign origins. Monsieur de Saint-Cotin was quite captivated by the phenomenon. He looked at the two young people and foresaw a union that would bring two ancient families close together. If the Marquis's treacherous brothers could ever be made to see sense, perhaps by force of arms, the Count himself would no longer have to depend on the charity of *his* own brother. The thought of not being beholden to the Lord of Tenebran was a sweet one indeed, but the Count kept it to himself for fear of anything going wrong.

Indeed, things were going so well by the end of lunch that when Serafin begged leave to be excused, the Marquis did not even notice her departure. The Count had already proposed a tour of the gardens to the Marquis and Mademoiselle Elisabeth, and so the three of them, followed only by three servants, made their way to the sunny walks outside.

His stomach full of good food, his head full of pleasant thoughts, the Marquis walked slowly with his new friends and spoke but little, leaving Monsieur to make most of the running. It was pleasant to be listened to for a change, Monsieur thought, as the image of his brother flitted into his mind, then out again. The Marquis seemed to be taking everything he said seriously. And Elisabeth walked in a dream by their side. He is no gilded fool, she told herself. He is nothing like any of the men I have ever met. I am sure his life will have been of the most interesting and unusual kind.

There were many other people in the gardens and much activity: gardeners, workers hammering away at something, an architect with unrolled plans. There were no other guests. Monsieur was telling the Marquis how the Lord of Tenebran had many rich friends but did not receive many guests, and then he could not stop himself from blurting out the amazing, terrifying event that was to happen a week or so hence.

"The King himself—yes, yes! You see that architect here? He is designing a pavilion to house the plays, operas, the magnificent light shows that will reveal to the King the splendors of Tenebran! The King himself will stay in the large room downstairs. It has already been altered, specially prepared. It will be an extraordinary thing, but . . ." He paused, and the other two stopped walking too.

"But?" said the Marquis in his musically foreign tones.

He is so perceptive, thought Monsieur in gratitude. He understands that I am uneasy. Elisabeth, too, regarded him with interest and understanding, and Monsieur's kindly heart swelled.

"You are right, my friend," he said. "*But* indeed."

The Marquis smiled encouragingly, and Monsieur, first looking to make sure no one was around, whispered: "It is perhaps dangerous. For who knows what the King may think?"

"Who knows, indeed," the Marquis said, nodding, and then started as a well-known voice issuing instructions to the workers drifted to him from the other side of the path.

Monsieur seemed not to notice his agitation, being consumed by his own. "I have said to my brother that . . ."

"Father." Elisabeth's tone carried a warning. As she spoke, they all saw a newcomer approaching them. Tall, dressed all in deep brown, with a curling moustache and a beauty spot at the corner of his mouth, he came toward them, his face cast in lines of politeness that denoted neither servant nor noble but someone in between.

Monsieur nodded to this man, his hands betraying a certain nervousness despite his determinedly haughty manner. "Ah, Monsieur Balze, you are well I trust? It is good to see the work proceeding. Yes, hmmm, yes."

"Very well, thank you. Your Grace is too kind," said the man, his brilliant pale eyes quite expressionless.

"Monsieur Balze, I would like to introduce the Marquis of Carabas, who is our guest at present." He waved distractedly at the Marquis, who bowed, but whose limbs felt the chill of the other man's pale eyes directed at him.

"Ah, yes, the Marquis of Carabas, indeed. Yes, fine place, Carabas."

"You know it, Monsieur Balze? Oh, it must be a splendid place," said Elisabeth suddenly, and as suddenly blushed, as three pairs of eyes were directed at her.

"Oh yes, I know it," said Balze, bowing, "and it is indeed, Mademoiselle, a most unusual and interesting place."

Meeting someone who knew his birthplace seemed to have struck the Marquis dumb with nostalgia. Monsieur, as eager to get away from Balze as he was sorry for the Marquis's apparent distress, said rather vaguely: "Well, well, time to be getting on. Nice to see you, Balze."

"If I can be of any help to the Marquis," the man called Balze said, "any help at all—why, he will know to call on me."

"Yes, yes, thank you," said Monsieur, even more vaguely, while the Marquis nodded, rather stiffly.

These middle classes, Elisabeth thought as they walked sedately away down the path. They do rather go on. As if Monsieur Balze has anything to offer the Marquis, she thought daringly.

The Marquis could feel the eyes still on his back. His heart thumped most unpleasantly. For a second, as he had looked into those blank eyes, the splendid scene around him had faded, and he had been in a place he did not wish to remember. Then Mademoiselle Elisabeth's glance had made him strong enough to reject the mocking recognition in Balze's eyes, and the enchantment of the beautiful place folded around him again.

"A strange fellow, that Balze," Monsieur said reflectively, shuddering a little. "Of the merchant class, I believe. Too close to my brother." He paused, and whispered again: "Sometimes I think he must be a spy. Perhaps for . . . for . . ." Then he clamped his lips tight shut. "In any case, let us not waste any more time on that nonsense. Come with us, dear Marquis, and let us show you the latest marvels of Tenebran: the grottoes of the nymphs." And talking most happily, unease firmly shelved, the little party made its way down the long walks in pleasant contemplation of mutual benefit and contentment.

» Ten «

Serafin had found a warm seat in the kitchen and a ready tongue in the second cook, a youngish man of an extremely gossipy disposition. While Serafin sat quietly eating a plate of very tasty leftovers, the cook talked at length about the castle and it's inhabitants.

"How old is this castle you ask? Well, about ten years or so, though I was not here then. I come from further north, you know. Yes, not far from Paris. I have heard it said that there were once four villages here where the castle stands. Well, it must have taken a long time to build then, though I've heard that 'twas not so long as you might think—the Lord of Tenebran must have employed thousands of workers and it was finished in just a few months! Yes, I know I've never heard of such speed before but the rich are different from you or I and who knows what he was able to offer people to work hard. Yes, he's a bachelor, the Lord of Tenebran, and they do say he came from nowhere and made his money and name no one knows how. Long before my time, that was. I am not sure where he lived before then because, as I say, I only came after the castle was built and they were looking for people to work here. No, no one who works here is local, we all come from outside. Monsieur Balze the steward hires us and he does not like the local people too much. The Lord's brother and niece came to live here not long after the castle was completed. Yes, I believe Madame the Countess died in childbirth and the child was left motherless, so the Lord himself offered this refuge. Oh yes, they do say as how the Lord is an ogre in human shape but I am not sure of that at all, though there are stories of how in his younger days there were a few people who disappeared around here—strange stories of bodies found. But none here, no, and anyway they are only stories. His family seem to be quite like everyone else if you ask me. He does not like to see many people, however, so perhaps that is why all sorts of stories are told of him. I could tell you a few but I won't as I'm too busy with this pastry. Antoine, come here, wash this dish. No, you blockhead, this one! But you know the Lord is getting more and more powerful. He has bought much land around and they do say as how his coffers are more fulfilled than those of the King himself. Ah, don't repeat that, will you, but you seem the kind who can keep a secret. The King—the King himself—will be coming here in a few days time, oh and what will we cook for him? Already we are planning, planning. But you ask about Monsieur. Oh, he is kept on a string by his brother and he knows which side his bread is buttered on that one."

Serafin, sitting there at ease in the warm, aromatic air of the kitchens, smiled. "And Monsieur Balze, I can see he is a man to be reckoned with. Not an easy man, eh?"

The cook looked at him, opened his mouth, and then closed it again. "You must be tired," he then suggested firmly. "All good for some, I dare say, who do only have a young whipper-snapper to look after and not a bunch of useless idle sods. An-toine! No! That is not for you. Oh, if first cook saw you! I do advise you, Monsieur Serafin, to get yourself some rest in the next few days, for there will be no rest when the King is here. Oh, and Monsieur Serafin—the upstairs left corridor rooms. That there are the Lord's. Only he may go there, and sometimes one of us bringing him meals. And even then we must leave it by the door. So do not go up there. It is not worth your while—and it is not a good place." He looked carefully at Serafin. "There was a boy, rather too curious, a few years ago, oh yes, and he went along and opened the door to the Lord's room and . . . Well, I know someone who found him outside there, stone dead, and there were no more brave excursions then, I can tell you." He turned decisively back to the kitchen boy. "Now then. Where did you put the ladle, idle useless good for . . . ?"

Grinning, Serafin left the kitchen.

» » « «

59

Inside the main body of the castle, there was the sound of hammering on the ground floor, in a section that had been completely blocked off to traffic. Some renovation going on for the King's visit, no doubt, thought Serafin. Everywhere, the decor spoke of riches and splendor on a scale Serafin could never have imagined: painted ceilings in gorgeous colors, richly covered furniture, even a wall of silver mirrors, creating endless reflections in the already spacious room. On the other side of the main vestibule was a large reception room. Next to that was the dining room where they had eaten previously and the suite of rooms belonging to the Count, which included the Marquis's room. At the very back was an enormous flight of stairs, all marble and gilt, and Serafin walked up them, soft-footed, unobserved (for whoever noticed where a cat went?). The stairs led up to a massive door that swung open surprisingly easily to the touch. Behind the door were a number of passageways running straight ahead and to the right and left.

Serafin hesitated only for a moment, then padded quietly over to the left. Being told not to do a thing always had the opposite effect on her. And this was part of her destiny. This was what the Law commanded. This was the other part of it, the part the peasants, the ordinary people, even the ordinary inhabitants of this enchanted castle, would never know about. This was the Law that sought out the Adversary, the Law that judged and condemned. This was the part that had been buried most deeply, the part that the young man with the old eyes had hinted at.

The corridor was very quiet. It was painted a soft gray with panels of gilt. Serafin found a door ajar and slipped in through the opening. The curtains were half-drawn, but it was possible to see that this was a bedchamber, with the most sumptuous furnishings Serafin had yet encountered. It was quite deserted, however. In size and shape the room resembled the Marquis's room downstairs, down to the little narrow annex off its side that housed a bed—not slept in, judging by its stern, unrumpled appearance—and a single chair with a coat hanging off it. Serafin walked to the coat, sniffed it delicately, and recoiled at the strange smell that rose from it.

Rapidly she walked out of the room and down the corridor again. Another door, again half-open. Carefully, carefully she pushed it back a little more and slipped unobserved into the room.

For a moment the gloom was too profound to see anything, but Serafin's eyes adapted to darkness easily, and soon shapes began to emerge. There was a musty, heavy smell in the room, something that caught at the nostrils and the throat. Slowly Serafin crept toward the figure by the window. The figure was perfectly still, looking uncannily like a statue, but Serafin knew it was no statue.

"Who is there?" The voice was weary, heavy—dusty, if a voice could be said to be dusty.

Serafin said nothing but moved closer to the figure.

"I can hear you, I can smell you, but I cannot see you."

Serafin shrank back a little as the figure lifted its shadowy head and peered into the darkness. Then it gave a gusty kind of sigh and rose, shuddering, to its feet. And now Serafin could see it more clearly.

It was a man, a man seemingly as tall as a young tree, with eyes that looked almost blind, and a great head of hair like a lion's. It was impossible to guess his age, for although the face was deeply scored, the hands seemed quite smooth. This man was dressed in clothes that looked curiously old-fashioned, and the musty smell Serafin had noticed previously clung about them.

"I had heard one was to come," the man said, and now there was a rumble of menace in the voice. "I have power greater than you can imagine, and could destroy you in seconds. So come out of the shadows. Show me yourself."

Serafin edged reluctantly out of the gloom. There was a silence, then a strange sound that was rather like a strangled sob. After a short time, Serafin became aware that the strange figure was *laughing*. The man did not sound as if he often laughed, and there was an odd threat in the disordered quality of it that sent a shiver rippling over Serafin's back.

"A cat! A cat, by my lord!" The man was laughing again, the harsh sound grating. "A cat! And this is what I was afraid of? This is the messenger of the Law?" A massive hand shot out and grabbed Serafin by the scruff of the neck. Two hooded, half-blind dark eyes stared straight into Serafin's. *Cat.* The word was a hiss of contempt. The man threw Serafin down and turned back to where he had been sitting. Serafin now saw that the man had been seated at a table, a table piled high with half-chewed bones and uncovered dishes.

"I am the great Lord of Tenebran," said the man, hollowly. "And you dare come into my presence. I have no doubt you are a *matagot,* one of those wonder cats beloved of our superstitious peasants."

For the first time, Serafin spoke. "Beware of pride."

"Pride?" The Lord of Tenebran laughed again, no less harshly than before. "Pride is all mine. Did you see my castle, my lands? Soon the King will visit, and he will see that I am richer than he. And then . . . well, we will see."

"Indeed," said Serafin dryly, and gathering for a spring, jumped up onto the table.

For a moment the Lord looked as if he would throw the cat down again, but instead he shrugged and picked up a chicken bone. "I knew long ago that one day a messenger of power would come and that would be the end for me. If power has such messengers, then I need not fear! Only if I were a mouse would you be a problem." He belched, laughed, and as he did so, Serafin became aware that the light in the room was growing, although the window was still curtained. Soon the chamber was flooded with light.

"So, Puss, what have you come to tell me?"

Serafin did not flinch. "To tell you the end is near, and you should prepare yourself." The words came from deep within the frail body, from deep within Serafin's divided nature, from the Law that had both made her and divided her. After a short silence, the Lord of Tenebran laughed, shortly.

"My dear Pusskins. You obviously do not seem to grasp that I am the great Lord of Tenebran. I am your Adversary. I have real power at my command. In an instant you would be dust if I chose so."

"If that is so, why were you so afraid when I came in?"

"I was not afraid. I am not used to being disturbed."

"If you have so much power, why do you stay here locked in the dark whilst the humblest of your servants is able to feel the sunshine and the breeze?"

"What need do I have of such things? From my room I can command anything, everything. See, I willed this light into the room. I willed all the prosperity and beauty of the countryside for my castle, and I even gave some to my foolish brother."

"If that is so, why do you not go out into that beauty?"

"'If that is so, if that is so,' you seem to know no other words. How did you come here?"

"I came as a messenger and a servant. I serve the Law, which will ensure your end."

"You speak with words too big for such a small animal. Look, I will show you what I am capable of!" With a roar the man flung up his arms, and the room filled with livid flashes of lightning. "See? I can command the powers of the earth."

"And who commands you?" Serafin, ears flattened, heart thumping, had nevertheless stayed put on the table during the terrifying display. "Who commands *you*, oh Lord of Tenebran? Who is your master?"

The big man dropped his arms, and the lightning faded away. He stood there looking at Serafin, his eyes full of a kind of madness. But he said nothing. For a fraction of a moment, Serafin held the man's gaze, then, without being molested, jumped down from the table and padded out of the door. Not a moment too soon, for footsteps were ringing rapidly on the marble floors, and a man was striding down the passageway toward the Lord's room.

» Eleven «

There was everything in this castle and its marvelous grounds to keep a young lady happy, the Count had often proclaimed to Elisabeth. Did she want fine clothes? Why, there were seamstresses who at a word could make the finest creations of spider's web lace and softest satin, milliners who could fashion the most extravagant hats of feathers and wicker, shoemakers who could cobble slippers of glass. Did she want fine food? There were cooks better than any to be found at Court, tirelessly confecting cakes as light as angels' breath, towers of spun sugar, dishes of surpassing excellence in every way. Did she want to take the air? There were one hundred and twenty walks to be had on marvelous grounds, and parties of ball games and ingenious sports that were invigorating but enabled a lady to keep her dignity. Did she want amusements? There were people devoted to providing light shows, conjurers of amazing power, singers of perfect pitch, actors who performed every day if required. Did she want food for the mind? There were philosophers and teachers aplenty, all with their own favored subject, all more learned than any to be found anywhere else on Earth. Did she want affection? She had her own dear father and her poor uncle who each doted on her and wished to make her life the most favored in the land.

But still, the Count had often thought gloomily as he surveyed his daughter, still it did not seem enough. He was not sure what was required to make this younger generation happy, to make their eyes dance with frank pleasure at being alive. Beautiful his daughter certainly was, but lifeless, until, that is, the Marquis came on the scene.

Monsieur looked with pleasure at his daughter and the Marquis, heads bent over some pretty flower in the garden. Really, the young man was most charmingly unworldly in many ways. Perhaps all French fathers should consider getting such unspoiled parish husbands for their daughters. If he did not know all the pretensions and niceties of aristocratic life here, what of it? Life in Spain was obviously very different indeed. As he surveyed the scene, pictures of the young man's imagined homeland filled the Count's head most pleasantly. It came to him, as he watched the two young lovers, that the setting in which they found themselves was altogether too formally perfect to be really beautiful. It was somehow unnatural, perhaps. This place where he had lived happily for over ten years now appeared to have a jaded quality in contrast to the energy and beauty of the young couple. Odd—it was almost as if the contentment of the young couple had brought an answering *discontentment* in him. His musings brought to the front of his mind all those questions, all those doubts that he always tried so hard to bury. How had this place been built so quickly? Where had his brother, like himself a member of a well-born but poor family, obtained the riches for such an undertaking? Why did they never see his brother these days except masked, as if something hideous had happened to his face? Who was Monsieur Balze *really*, and why did he seem as much master as servant? But no, that question must never be asked, even silently. Monsieur promptly pushed these unpleasant thoughts out of his head and concentrated on feeling pleased at the pretty sight of two lovebirds.

The Marquis and Elisabeth felt no such conflict. The Marquis could quite easily imagine himself and Elisabeth living there happily ever after, lots of children to come, and Serafin too growing older, contented, that strange white hair hidden under a wig. He thought of his previous life as a dream from which he had awoken to his rightful place in the universe. God was good, the world was good, and best of all was the thought of the future. It stretched before him, golden and joyful. He would make Elisabeth happy, for, as her father had noted, he was unworldly, and did not even know that aristocrats thereabouts fashionably scorned such things of the heart, unless they could be mocked in pretty verses.

Elisabeth, for her part, felt also as if she had awoken from a dream. A dream stickily set about with lovely traps, a dream of unreality. *This* was real: the Marquis's hands, so charmingly slender against the milky whiteness of his sleeves; the Marquis's eyes, so feelingly fixed on her. For the first time, the gardens, the castle became real too, and not just the conjuration of a fairy tale. The flowers really grew here, in soil that smelled of sun and rain. The pale stone of the castle was warm to the touch, the rituals of castle life full of meaning now that the Marquis shared them. She was no longer anxious for the future, no longer full of vague disquiets. Even the sight of Monsieur Balze with his piercing eyes, even the thought of her uncle so terrifyingly isolated did not make her shrink. She was full of the bravery of her new feelings, full of the courage of the young when the world seems tuned to their own desires.

And she thought that the crowning moment would come when the King arrived, for she and the Marquis would by then have announced to her father and her uncle that they planned to marry, and the King would bless them.

>> >> << <<

Serafin, back in human shape, caught sight of the picture the three of them presented and grinned, without amusement but with a certain kindness nevertheless. Let them think everything was fine, let them rest for a while in the pleasure of their thoughts. It was not their fault if they were stupid, and intelligence was not always either a sign of goodness or a guarantee of happiness. Quite the opposite often, in fact. Serafin's past life was not a dream, but neither was this one. As Catou she had been uncertain, resentful, anxious. Now, just like the Marquis, she had become someone quite other, someone more on the road to her destiny. Unlike him, however, she was aware of all that she had once been and all that she was now. She had not forgotten that the Law must be fulfilled, right down to the last question.

But she must wait now for the next move, could not precipitate anything. Her coming had been observed, noted, understood, even if not fully. Her experience in the "ogre's" chamber had reinforced her knowledge that her opponent was indeed dangerous and had not yet been properly revealed. She had been rather surprised by the crudity of the Lord of Tenebran's arguments—power, commands—but then that was to be expected. He was of the same family as Monsieur and Elisabeth, after all. Despite his protestations, he was not the real Adversary, she was sure of that. But she must beware of complacency, of pride, even as she had warned him against it, for he was dangerous, there was no doubt of that.

Serafin walked in the perfumed gardens, noting that despite the buzz of activity, the workmen were uncharacteristically silent. Building sites usually rang with oaths and songs and sudden anger; this one was so busy, so intent on activity, that it was odd. If the steward usually employed such unnatural marvels of workmen, it was no wonder that the castle had been completed so quickly. She watched for a moment as the workers turned what had been a pretty alcove into a stage shaped like an egg, with a background gilded and garlanded and a platform made of light curved wood. "I'll wager you have never seen such a thing before."

The voice made her start a little. Serafin turned and saw a tall man with wheat-colored hair and glittering eyes. She shrugged. "No."

"And you must be Monsieur Serafin."

"Yes. And you must be Monsieur Balze."

"Of course. You will have heard of me."

No question, that. Serafin, still looking at the workmen, murmured, "Who has not?"

"Who has not, indeed? But you, Serafin: who has heard of *you?* I knew your mother once. A stubborn woman. Stupidly so. I offered . . ."

"I know what you offered. She told me."

"And how did her refusal profit her? She died, like the others. She could no longer protect you. What good is your Law then?"

"It is the Law."

"A stubborn, stupid one too, eh, Serafin? You will finish like your mother. And I . . . well, I will always be there, and you will not."

"We chose, long ago. We do not go back on the Law."

"But I do. I did, long ago, and do so every day. And look where I am. And look at you, Serafin. Long ago your people chose badly. And what are you now? Neither of here nor of there. Condemned to borderlands always. And for what? For those who have no understanding of you. It is stupid."

"Perhaps. But that is how we are."

"Look at me, Serafin. Really look at me, with your own eyes, not the blinkered ones of the Law. Stop thinking of me as the Adversary. Look."

She could not stop herself from looking at him, straight into those eyes, and saw there worlds that called to her so sweetly that she flinched. In the depths of those strange-colored eyes, she saw eternal life, boundless joy, power to do with as she willed, beauty everlasting.

"You see?" he said softly.

She forced her eyes away. "I see. But I do not see price."

"Price? Price? You talk as if you were like *them*, bound to Earth with questions of value and price. Shop talk. Unworthy."

"I am bound to Earth. Don't you remember that I am at least half of Earth? And we chose, as I said, long ago."

"That is of no account. Your true nature is not of Earth. It cannot be, and you know that." He paused, and went on, "In any case, what you see before you is of no account. They in the castle are a mere nothing. Who will remember them a hundred years from now? If you bind yourself to the earth, to your human half, think deeply. You will suffer their human fate too. If you bind yourself finally, you will be bound by all the laws of Earth. You will no longer be able to change your shape or know the future or the reality behind all things. You will be merely human dust."

"And if I do not?" Her voice was almost inaudible.

"If you do not bind yourself? Why, you have seen that for yourself. Who would exchange that for dust?"

"But how many have chosen that, in the end?"

"That is of no account. What does it matter, how many have chosen, how many have been stupid enough to prefer death to eternal life?"

For the first time since the beginning of their conversation, Serafin felt a lifting of the heart. "So none have chosen your way."

"I did not say that." There was a touch of anger in the smooth, cool voice. "You put words in my mouth. Remember, Serafin, Catou, however you call yourself. Remember what the villagers, who had known you all your life, wanted to do to you. Remember how your stupid boy has regarded you with suspicion and fear, despite all you have done for him. See how he forgets you now, how quickly he becomes other than what he was. That is humanity."

But a memory had returned to her, and she stared at him. "It was your voice, in the village, urging them on. It was you."

"They did not need me. Oh yes, I play with them, for they are but diversions: human dust, as I said. I do not need wealth and power, they are nothing to me. But the villagers had not needed me to learn hate against you. I can only work with what is there, after all. I did not put it there. Think of that, Serafin. Your precious Law—is it really what you think it is? And your precious Marquis, or whatever it is he believes himself to be, has he told you that he met me—twice? Has he even breathed a word to you of his secret doubts, his contempt for you?"

"It was you," Serafin repeated, trying to hold Balze's voice at bay. "You."

"A bad habit, repeating words. You are dull, my dear. I do not know why I waste my time." He shrugged petulantly. "I have better things to do; for instance, supervising this work, in this castle, this place of enchantment, this place in which you all are sharing—because of *me*. We will resume another day, when you have come to your true senses, your true destiny." And with an arrogant flick of an elegant wrist, he was gone.

» Twelve «

"Marquis! Marquis!" The Count was—unwisely in a person of his station, not to mention girth—running. "Marquis!"

The Marquis was in his room, dreaming of Elisabeth, trying to memorize the courtly words Serafin had composed for him the night before. Serafin had promised that she would teach the young man to read, but the Marquis was not the quickest of students and the lessons were a trial. The Marquis did not know how his servant had learned such an arcane craft, and was rather annoyed that Serafin would not simply, by some magical method, instantly endow him with the skill to know and compose words. They had argued about it, and the Marquis had finally come to the idea that perhaps in Spain it was not necessary for nobles to read. Perhaps Elisabeth would simply see it as another of his charming eccentricities and the matter would then be resolved.

Serafin had smiled at that: yes, Elisabeth would no doubt enjoy being the one who organized business and daily affairs, as you needed to read for that. She looked like she would have a better head for it than the Marquis, who had yawned with relief and said yes, that would suit him fine, and that he was tired and wanted to go to sleep. First, though, Serafin had insisted on teaching him some tasty phrases to regale his lady with, for words were important to ladies, not just actions and pretty glances.

Now the Marquis was interrupted in his early practice of these words by his prospective father-in-law, who puffed in with his kindly face as red as the coat he wore that morning.

The Marquis was solicitous. "Do please sit down, Sir." He pulled out the most comfortable chair, which was nevertheless as stiff as a post and about as welcoming.

The Count gingerly lowered himself onto it. "My dear Marquis, such news! Monsieur Balze has brought me word, from my brother, that I am to go to Court for the day to receive final instructions on all that the King requires before he is to come here. And you are to come with me!"

"To Court? The King?" The Marquis suddenly felt faint. He too sat down, on his stiff and fastidiously made-up bed.

"Yes! Is that not exciting?"

"And will Mademoiselle Elisabeth . . . ?"

"Oh yes, she may go too, though Monsieur Balze says we are to be careful as the King has an eye—and more than an eye, oh yes—for a pretty girl. But we will take her to the Queen's apartments where my brother says she will be made welcome."

"A wonderful day."

The Marquis is as white as milk, thought the Count kindly. He is as overwhelmed as I am.

The Marquis was indeed overwhelmed. For a moment he was Frederic again, terrified as much as astonished by his good fortune. Too much, it was too much. Could it last? He, the youngest son of a miller, would be presented to the King of France! But the moment passed very quickly, so that he was almost unaware of it a second later.

"Now we must make sure you have the finest clothes possible. We are to leave at midday, as we are expected for the royal supper this evening, and we will return tomorrow at midday. I will instantly alert the dressers and the barbers so that all of us will look our best. Oh, and Monsieur Serafin may come with us too, as well as my own valet and my daughter's maid. There will be plenty of other servants at Court for all our other needs. Now hurry, my dear Marquis. We have little time—only four hours in which to get dressed and barbered, so you will have to hurry!"

And as abruptly as he had come in he went out again, his heels clicking on the floors, his large rear end waddling comfortably.

"Well, well." Serafin emerged from the side room. The Marquis was silent, lost in contemplation. "You will have to *hurry*, Marquis."

"Hurry? Yes." Like a sleepwalker, the Marquis got up and began wandering around the room. "The Court. The King. My God, Serafin!"

"I do not believe God will be there too," observed Serafin dryly. "However, yes, I do agree that this is indeed exciting news."

"I have heard of the Court, and the King," went on the Marquis in a dreamy voice, as if he had not even heard Serafin. "I have heard of his face, which shines like the sun, and of his palace, which is the most splendid the world has seen. I have heard that angels sang at his birth and that the heavens themselves rejoiced." Serafin muttered something. "What did you say? You doubted it? Oh, Serafin, stop being so boring, so ordinary, so *Earthbound!*"

"You are not the first to have told me so," said Serafin, without a smile. "However, we are going to Court. And you must make a good impression on the King. *I* have heard that he is a very quick judge of people, so first impressions count for a lot. Now, I will go and see what clothes we can find for you and make sure the barber and hairdresser make their way to you. Wait here for me. I will return very shortly."

Left alone, the Marquis tried to compose his thoughts by trying to bring to mind the phrases Serafin had taught him. But he could not. They seemed to have vanished like snow after rain. So he paced instead, up down up down, now and then pausing to glance in the mirror at the young man reflected there. It was not that he was vain, it was simply that he was innocently pleased with his transformation from miller's son to great noble and could not quite get over his amazement. He thought of Serafin, briefly, with an affection he did not question, and of Elisabeth, at length, with a contentment he could not quite repress, and he gave a little skip of pure delight.

"You have heard the news, then." Monsieur Balze, sleek as ever, stood in the doorway. "What an honor!"

"Indeed." He instantly felt uncomfortable, even though Monsieur Balze had so far not given so much as the tiniest hint that he had recognized the Marquis from their earlier meetings. "A great honor."

"And so you must look your best." The steward smiled. "Fine clothes, fine footwear."

"You are going yourself, Monsieur Balze?"

"Ah no, I fear not. Too much work here. But I will certainly be thinking of you."

"That is kind."

"Kind, yes." There was laughter in the steward's eyes, and the Marquis turned his own eyes away uneasily. "I have something here that I believe may be a fitting gift for the King."

"A gift? Of course! Oh, I had not considered that. You are most thoughtful . . ."

"I know how hard it must be for you being so far away from home and having had to leave in such difficult circumstances," went on the steward, gravely. "And I know that things are different where you come from, and you may not know that no one goes to see the King without a gift. I am sure that in Spain, kings give rather than receive, yes? But here in France our kings do like their presents."

The Marquis, aware of being mocked but mesmerized by the man's smooth manner, said nothing.

Monsieur Balze nodded gently, and said, holding out a small parcel: "So here is something. A small curiosity for the great King." The Marquis took the parcel. "Oh, please look," said the steward, detecting the Marquis's hesitation. "You must know what it is, if you are to be the giver of such a gift." And he watched as the young man unfolded the rich cloth that had been wrapped around the object, and nodded as the other's eyes widened at the sight before him.

"I have some skill with wood," he said with feigned modesty as the Marquis gazed in delight at the most beautiful little box he had ever seen, carved with exquisite workmanship, inlaid with ebony and ivory and gems. Gently, he opened the little catch.

The interior was lined in purple silk, with a little round mirror set in the lid. He was about to peer into the mirror when Monsieur Balze reached over and closed the box again.

"Is it a gift fit for a King then, the mirrored box of heart's desire?" Balze's eyes were dancing.

The Marquis nodded, not really listening at all. "*Some* skill with wood? This is of such beauty as I have never . . ."

"I have many talents." Monsieur Balze seemed impatient. "Now wrap it away again and carry it safely on yourself. I'll wager the King will be pleased with you. Oh, and perhaps you could keep this as our secret, yes?"

The Marquis nodded, dumbly. He rolled up the box again in the cloth, very carefully, and put it in the pocket of his brocade dressing gown.

"You are so kind," he managed at last. "Is there anything I can do to thank you?"

The steward looked at him, a smile playing at the corner of his fine mouth. "It will be enough for me to think of the thing I made going to the greatest king in the world. And now, Marquis, I must go. I hope you will enjoy your day at Court, and I look forward to hearing about it on your return."

» Thirteen «

Really, thought Monsieur de Saint-Cotin, as the coach lurched on its way over the bumpy roads, the coachman stopping now and then to tighten reins or check the wheels. Really, this was the most wonderful day of his life. Or at least till the next one—the one he dared not quite picture yet, when the Marquis would marry his daughter in splendor at Tenebran, watched by the King himself. He watched the young people as they swayed in time to the coach's motion, the Marquis whispering things to Elisabeth that sometimes made her color prettily, and his tender heart was touched.

He thought of his dead wife, Louise, God rest her soul, and of how he and she had courted. So soft and sweet she was, he thought, on the verge of tears, forgetting her sharp glances and not-always-sugared tongue. But she had been kind to him, had never mocked him as so many had done. He had been a bumbling fat boy from the start, and other children had played tricks on him—tricks that bewildered him, for he had no malice, no resentment of the world. His parents had died within a few months of each other, leaving him with little money but the honor of a great and ancient name. It was only then that he had learned he had a brother, or rather a half brother, a man who had become the Lord of Tenebran. It was not long after he had become engaged to Louise that his brother had come to find him, saying he had no heirs and Monsieur no money so the two should work well together. It was as if a magic wand had been waved over his life—acquiring a love and a family and a fine life-style all at once.

But Louise had not liked his brother much, although she had tried to do so for his sake. Like all women, she was fanciful and had conceived the notion that the Lord of Tenebran was a sinister figure. When she was alive, they had not visited Tenebran very much, and certainly Louise had insisted on never staying there overnight.

His brother had not taken offense; no, quite the contrary. When Monsieur was widowed, his brother had suggested he come to live at Tenebran, a suggestion Monsieur had agreed to with great relief. And certainly since then he'd been proven right. His brother had looked after their every need. They never wanted for anything, and his daughter had been brought up in a manner befitting her rank. But occasionally, especially in the hours just before dawn, Monsieur would awaken with unease gripping his limbs.

He had learned to deal with that, but dealing with his brother had become more and more difficult over the years. Sometimes Monsieur was frightened at the changes in him that had appeared over time, but he reassured himself that being the lord of a vast estate was of course very worrying, and thanked heaven that he did not have to be put through such trials.

More and more he was getting his instructions through Monsieur Balze. This saved him from seeing the pitiful state of his brother, of course, but was in itself a source of some disturbance. Though there was nothing in the man's manner that could possibly give offense, Monsieur had never liked the steward, with his too-knowing eyes.

But now Carabas had arrived, and that had changed everything. Somehow the young man had made many of Monsieur's problems seem unreal and far away. Monsieur Balze had reported that Monsieur's brother was pleased at the young man's entry into their society, and at the effect on Elisabeth. It had, so the steward reported, given great pleasure to the Lord of Tenebran. And that had warmed Monsieur's heart, for he dearly wanted his brother to be happy.

Monsieur de Saint-Cotin was still lost in his reverie when the coach came to a village, and the coachman stopped to check the wheels again. Through the half-open window came the sound of music.

"Oh!" The Marquis already had his head out of the carriage and was looking at the village. He ducked his head back in. "A wedding!" he said. His cheeks had suddenly gone pink under their powder. "Oh, look!"

Elisabeth and Monsieur put their heads out discreetly. It would not do to seem too interested in the activities of villagers, but the Marquis's obvious pleasure was charming. So they looked, and they saw long tables set up in a square, people sitting around them eating and drinking, and, under a tree, two musicians—one with violin, one with bagpipes—playing for all they were worth. People were dancing near them, women with skirts flying, men with hips swinging, and there was raucous laughter.

"Interesting," said Monsieur, "the pleasures of simple folk." But the Marquis was not listening at all. Murmuring, "Wait, wait a moment," he had jumped out of the coach and was striding toward the dancers. Astonished, Elisabeth stared at her father, who stared back, quite at a loss. What was going to happen now?

Watching with round eyes, they saw the Marquis reach the dancers. They saw, too, his servant, Serafin, go after him. They saw Serafin talking to him and then saw the Marquis stride away from him. They saw the Marquis begin to dance in vigorous steps, keeping perfectly in time with the music. They saw the astonishment, then fear, then delight of the villagers, who crowded around this dancer in his fine clothes. They saw the Marquis twirling and stamping, and they looked at each other.

"In Spain things must be very different," said Monsieur, but then found he was speaking to empty air, for Elisabeth had wrenched open the door and gone out in her turn, running quite without dignity to the group clustered around the dancer. And her amazed father saw her lift her skirts and begin dancing too—one, two, three, four, hop—quite as if she belonged there.

"Well, this is really most extraordinary," said Monsieur, as he watched their activities and saw how Serafin had stopped at the edge of the group and was watching them too. "This is really most extraordinary," he repeated as he hurried out of the coach and toward them. "Really most unheard of," he murmured, as he was swept into the flood of joyful dancers by a tall thin woman with a beaklike nose.

"But we are going to see the King," he called out in a lull, as the Marquis swept by him, arm in arm with his daughter.

"But we dance first, we dance first!" answered that truly extraordinary young man, and indeed he did not stop dancing for a good long while, long after Monsieur had been helped to a bench, panting and almost purple.

Strangely, though, Monsieur felt more at rest than he had in many long years, and he watched without resentment as the vigorous youngsters danced on and on. He beckoned to Serafin. "One would think your master had been born to this kind of dancing!"

"In Carabas, this is what people do," said the poker-faced servant.

"Nobles dancing with villagers?"

"Oh yes. It is considered very bad form to look down on those less fortunate."

"I see. Yes, of course." Serafin had a very magisterial manner, and Monsieur was rather impressed by it. He certainly could think of no reason why this state of affairs in Carabas should not be so. It would not do for our lands, he thought, but people elsewhere have their own thoughts. This feeling reconciled him quite to the extraordinary idea. In fact, the more he thought about it, the better it seemed, so that he said to Serafin: "We will give these good people, these people whose wedding it is, a token of affection. Please be so good as to fetch my purse from the coach, Monsieur Serafin."

"Very good, Monsieur," said Serafin, bowing slightly and smiling.

Monsieur turned back to watch the dancers, his heart swelling with fellowship. Ah, really, life was a strange thing, for noble or villager, and those who saw too much difference were truly not seeing with their eyes.

》 》 《 《

The young bridal couple were touchingly grateful for the two gold louis that Monsieur recklessly gave them. They behaved as if they had never held one of these coins before, a truly charming display of gratitude. The other villagers were silent at this, no doubt overcome with pleasure and joy for them. When Monsieur, the Marquis, and Elisabeth bade farewell to them, they stood in silent ranks, their eyes full of emotion. It made Monsieur feel quite wobbly with the sense of good accomplished. As they drove away, someone in the crowd shouted out something in a village tongue Monsieur did not understand, but which the Marquis obviously did, for he started a little and colored.

"You understand these people? Is their dialect similar to your own?" Monsieur said, in some surprise.

The Marquis made a deprecating gesture, then said, "Yes, that is so."

"Interesting," murmured Monsieur. "Perhaps there was once close contact between Carabas and France." He smiled. "As there is again now."

"That's right," said the Marquis, his own smile a little shaky.

"What did they say? Words of thanks? Astonishment?"

"Yes."

"They are good people. You know, Marquis, I think that this idea of your people, that noble and villager should not have so many barriers between them as we do in France, is a good idea. It is pleasant to feel one has lightened their lives today. Pleasant to feel that God's creatures are all one."

But the Marquis seemed disinclined to talk. No doubt he was tired. Monsieur was not upset by this. He could understand. And he was grateful to the Marquis for opening his eyes thus far. Besides, the coachman had told him they had made good time, and that even with this unexpected break, they would arrive at Court in plenty of time. His head full of pleasant thoughts, his limbs pleasantly relaxed, lulled by the motion of the coach, Monsieur de Saint-Cotin fell into a gentle sleep.

» Fourteen «

Their first sight of the palace of the Sun King was from the vantage point of a narrow, rather muddy road leading into the gates of the palace proper. Much of it was a building site, for the King had started on alterations that would take years to complete and that would turn it into the most magnificent palace the world would ever see. The buildings—square, low, and elegant in the style of the previous century—were being transformed into a setting worthy of the greatest king who had ever lived.

To our friends, used to the splendors of Tenebran, the palace looked rather ordinary. It was set in the middle of pleasant orcharded and cultivated lands, with low hills in the distance. A circular, low-walled enclosure led up to the gates, and it was there that the coach stopped and the whole party got out. The coach and horses were driven away to one of the many stables attached to the palace, and the group was taken in charge by a man who had approached them unsmiling, his manner as stiff as brocade.

"Good evening. We bid you welcome, and ask you please to follow me."

Each of them immediately felt the terror and excitement of the impending future, when they would be face to face with the King himself: Monsieur felt a familiar gripping in the stomach, and fussed needlessly over the ribbons on his coat; Elisabeth, who had heard of the King's reputation despite the best efforts of her father, felt her heart skip a beat; the Marquis felt his heart thudding in his chest, for surely he was now at the center of the world; even Serafin felt a quickening of the pulse.

Then the man made an imperious gesture, and the great wrought-iron gates opened. Sentries stood on either side, their eyes blank and cold. In front of the visitors were graveled walks and lakes, and beyond, the buildings where the King of France lived and worked.

Their guide walked them past groups of courtiers, who gazed at the group with an air of insolence. They were seeing all types entering these gates, something that surely would not have happened with other kings, they told themselves. But Louis had his own peculiar ideas and had even appointed commoners to positions of power. Naturally they never expressed their resentment to their King. Instead, they took out their feelings on the provincials who came to Court every day on some stupid errand or the other. Now, the unhappy Monsieur heard several quite clear remarks on the old-fashioned nature of his clothes—remarks that could only be ill-natured because he knew his clothes to be in the latest style. They criticized his daughter's coloring too, but strangely enough the Marquis seemed to pass muster, with several remarks being passed on his "natural, obvious grace." One or two ladies even ventured meaningful smiles at the young man, but Monsieur was pleased to see that the Marquis did not even seem to notice them. They have too little to do, these people, he thought indignantly. Unlike me, with an estate and a daughter and a brother to worry about, these courtiers have nothing to do. And he was pleased to recall that the King reportedly thought them a pack of gilded fools, feathered idiots to be kept in the cage of Court, for they would never survive in the real world.

At last they were out of the range of the spiteful, and their guide—who had shown no sign of noticing either the remarks or the courtiers—led them to a small building to one side, and then up a flight of stairs to a suite of rooms.

"These are to be your quarters for tonight," he said, his voice coming out in the kind of rusty croak of one who rarely used his vocal cords. "Your servants have antechambers leading off yours. You are to be ready for your audience with the King at six o'clock sharp. And then there will be the supper. In the meantime you are welcome to visit the gardens and the public rooms. If you need any help, please use this bell. A servant will attend to you." And with a slight bow, he was gone.

» » « «

Serafin, liberated by a rather embarrassed Marquis from brushing his clothes and shoes, was sitting quietly in the plain room allocated to her. The episode in the village had both tired and depressed her, for it had made her wonder, for the first time, why it was that she had to follow the Law to the end. Would Frederic really be happier as the Marquis, his past gone, his only identity a false one, one of enchantment? It would gain him—it had already gained him—riches and an ease beyond compare with his old life, but what would that profit him in the end? Would he become another Monsieur: a silly, empty-handed fool, blinded by his own fatuousness? Or worse still, like a Lord of Tenebran: a shell of a man guarding his great powers, already so in thrall to the Adversary that he was barely human any longer? When she had seen him in the middle of the villagers, dancing, belonging with them, she had heartily wished she possessed real magic rather than shape-shifting and mere conjuring, magic of the kind that would whisk him back to his old life unaware that he had even left it. But did he really belong with the villagers now? Besides, there was Elisabeth. They would be happy, those two.

It seemed a heavy burden for her, for Serafin, that she could not be freed from the obligation until the Law was complete. And the Law involved a terrible trial for the Marquis, as well as for Serafin, although she was not as yet sure of what it would be. She had not been granted perfect foreknowledge, because that would interfere with the proper functioning of the Law.

She thought of her conversation with Monsieur Balze and shivered a little. His eyes knew many things. Did they hold the knowledge of what would happen? If so, they were all as good as doomed.

"Serafin!" The Marquis's voice was rather more imperious than it had been in his days as Frederic. Rebellion fluttered in

83

Serafin's heart, but she got up, wearily. It was odd, really, how the young man had so easily become someone else, as if he were pulling on a glove. Even her own identity had changed for him. He never thought of her as female, as Catou, any longer. She was he now: Serafin, his discreet Spanish servant. It was really odd how humans, full humans, accepted such things without a qualm. It made her feel afraid, for surely such weak beings could never face the kinds of trials the Law had in store. She felt the contempt rising in her, and pushed it down, for once it took root in her, it could never be pulled out.

"Here I am," she replied.

The Marquis looked up at his servant in the doorway and said, in some agitation, "Serafin, have you any idea how one gives a gift to a king?"

Serafin had certainly not expected this one. "A gift? To a king? Why . . . why, like for anyone else, only more abased. 'Your Gracious, Golden Majesty, kindly accept this small token from your most humble, etc., etc.' Bows, scrapes, licking of shoes—only pretend, you understand. This king does not like real licking and scraping. He does not like spit on his beautiful gold satin shoes. It is so hard to clean off!"

The Marquis smiled. "You are absurd, Serafin. So you think if I simply bow and hand it over with a small word or two, that should be enough?"

"Why, I should think so. I should think anyway that the King has so many presents he has not even seen one-quarter of them." Then Serafin frowned. "But what gift are you giving him? Did Monsieur give you . . . ?"

"Yes, yes." The Marquis seemed eager to change the subject. "Good, thank you, Serafin. That will be all."

Serafin was never afterward sure if it was that dismissal or the Marquis's subsequent impatient turning to his mirror that made the difference. But the rebellion that had fluttered in her heart now flapped into full life. What was the use of her own devotion to the happiness of this idiot? With a curt, "You had better be careful. The time approaches," she spun on her heel and stalked from the room, uncaring of the Marquis's anger and dismay behind her. She went out into the gardens, keeping well away from the courtiers, and walked and walked and walked, her heart and her mind burning with the injustice of her destiny.

» Fifteen «

The King sat in a high-backed carved chair, his right arm resting on a table covered with a rich tapestry, his left hand holding a gold-tipped cane. He was well formed, with dark curling hair, blue eyes set in a round face, and a small moustache over firm, thin lips. He was dressed in red and silver and blue, the brocade of his coat picked out in the finest silver thread, his legs beautifully shaped in their red stockings, his breeches and shoes of silver silk and satin. His wife, the Queen, was not present at this occasion, Louis having declared that such functions bored her. Behind him stood dark-wigged gentlemen in clothes not quite as splendid as his, and below the dais where he sat were rows of courtiers who watched behind fans and well-bred hands as people ascended the steps and fell to their knees before the King. It was hard to see what Louis was feeling, for his soft young face was carefully set, his eyes the eyes of a statue, or a picture.

"The Marquis of Carabas and Monsieur de Saint-Cotin!" announced the royal guard who had brought them in. The courtiers craned their necks to see, expecting to be diverted by the spectacle of provincials who would probably stumble on the steps. Royal audiences could be dull indeed. Behaving as if you were in a fine oil painting was all very well, but it made for a stiff neck and stifled yawns.

It was only a little way from the door to the dais, but as the Marquis and Monsieur advanced on the magnificent carpet, they felt as if they were crossing a limitless desert. It was bad form to look straight ahead at the person of the King; it was equally bad form to drop your eyes to the ground and wish yourself into the woven forest of the carpet. There was little to do but fix your gaze on some point to the right of the King, a gaze shrewd enough to prevent yourself from tripping up but not so direct- ed that the gentleman in line with your vision felt unduly target- ed. Monsieur, of course, had been born to these niceties, but the Marquis, through sheer fright, had hit upon the right note as well.

They made it safely to the dais, and Monsieur dropped onto one knee, murmuring words of praise and awe to the blank-faced young man who was, as everyone knew, the hub of the universe. His words were accepted with a slight nod, a slight lifting of one eyebrow, but otherwise the King could have been carved of stone. Then it was the Marquis's turn. Dropping on one knee, his heart thudding so loudly that he was sure every- one must hear him, he said, "Although I am from a foreign land, Your Majesty, I have heard tales of your great Court and I am deeply honored to be here." Louis nodded. He looked bored.

"I have a gift," the Marquis went on. He felt in his pocket for the box Monsieur Balze had given him. "It is only a small token, unworthy of your greatness, but in foreign lands, exiled from your presence . . ."

The King waved impatiently, but said nothing. It was left to one of the gentlemen around him, a tall individual with a frame like a scarecrow, to say, quietly but distinctly, "The King is not in- terested in flattery. Give your gift."

"Yes. Of course." The Marquis flushed bright red, and the courtiers giggled: at last, a small diversion. The Marquis held out the box. He was so flustered that he could not say anything at all. The gentleman who had spoken pointed at the tapestry- covered table beside the King. The Marquis scrambled clumsily to his feet, adding to the courtiers' amusement, and placed the box carefully on the table. The King, still looking bored, glanced at it and then picked it up. He turned it over in his hands, and every- one held their breath. As he did so, a sleek black shape insinuat- ed itself around his legs, mewing and purring. The King stared at it, and the courtiers gasped. Fancy interrupting the King! Even a mere cat should know not to do such a thing.

The King frowned. He raised an eyebrow at the scarecrow gentleman, who thundered, "Who does this cat belong to? Why is it in here?"

There was a murmur of denial, then a lady's languid voice drawled, "I saw this cat at the heels of the Marquis of Carabas, before he entered this hall." She smiled. "It appeared to be firm-ly attached to him."

"But I . . ." the Marquis stammered. "I do not have a . . ." He fell silent not because he was afraid, but because he had caught a familiar glare in the cat's eyes that startled him beyond measure. Then he noticed something that the courtiers had not yet seen. Around the cat's neck was a silver ribbon, on which something hung. The King saw this in the same moment, and his eyes—no longer bored and blank, but searching, intelligent, and dangerous—met those of the Marquis. Then he waved a hand at the scarecrow gentleman, who himself flapped at the noisy crowd. "Silence!"

Silence fell while everyone waited in delighted anticipation to see what would happen to the foolhardy owner of the tres-passing cat.

The King bent down to the animal. The courtiers saw him stroke the cat softly, carefully under the chin, and those closest to him heard him murmur something to it. Then he gently untied the silver ribbon and the object it bore and held them in his hand. The box, meanwhile, lay unregarded on the table.

Everyone waited. The Marquis had his eyes fixed on the cat, which was standing as bold and straight as you please.

Then the King spoke. "Your gift pleases us." He spoke bald-ly, without flowery ornamentation, and called himself "we," for he was the King, and that meant at least ten ordinary mortals. He smiled. "And we like your way of delivering it."

"The box, Your Majesty?" said the poor Marquis, feeling greatly daring and greatly in the dark.

"Box?" The King cast an indifferent glance at the beautiful little object on the table. "No. We have seen such things before. But this what your servant the cat brought." He smiled. "We think we shall have to knight your cat."

The Marquis did not dare say that he did not own the cat, had never seen it before. A frightening thought as to what the cat actually was had penetrated his innocent brain. He mumbled, "I am so glad to have brought a little pleasure to Your Majesty." He was rather at a disadvantage, not even knowing what the cat had brought the King of France, the Light of the World.

The King stroked the cat again, and laughed as it turned around and licked him on the hand. "Even humble beasts flatter us," he said jovially. "This must stop."

There was a ripple of laughter around the Court at this piece of wit. Even Monsieur, who had remained frozen to the spot during all this dangerous scene, joined anxiously in the merriment. It seemed that somehow the Marquis had pulled off a coup. What a man he was! How extraordinary! Monsieur had had no idea that he would do anything like this! He had taken a grave risk, yes, but he had somehow managed to make it an advantage. "Our people tell us you are at Tenebran at the moment," the King went on. He paused, seeming to wait for a comment from the Marquis, who nodded overeagerly, much to the malicious satisfaction of the courtiers, who were already feeling annoyed by this foreigner's success with the Sun King. But the King did not even seem to notice this breach of protocol. With another smile, he said, "And we will be glad to visit there in the near future. Tell the Lord of Tenebran that as well as being the Marquis of Carabas, you will also receive a French honor."

"Your . . . Your Majesty . . ." The Marquis's head spun, his legs trembled. He glanced at the cat, which seemed almost to grin. Then the King waved a hand, and his face closed again. The audience was over.

As the Marquis and Monsieur made their unsteady way back down the hall, the cat trotted at their heels, tail held high, and the murmurs from the courtiers followed the little group: "What was that he gave the King? What an extraordinary thing! What is the world coming to?" And so it went on, for there is nothing more galling to people of that sort than to think they do not know everything there is to gossip about.

» »   « «

Monsieur tried to discover what it was the Marquis had given the King, but the Marquis was quite infuriatingly quiet about it. It was almost as if the box had really been what he had intended to give the King. Such discretion both impressed and annoyed Monsieur, for if the Marquis were to be his son-in-law, surely he should not hide such important things.

When they returned to their rooms, the cat was no longer with them. They had not seen where it had gone, so intent had each been on their good fortune and their uneasy questions. But Serafin was in her antechamber, calmly folding clothes and seemingly quite unfazed by all the Marquis rather breathlessly recounted. When the Marquis had gone to find Elisabeth and ask her how her audience with the Queen had gone, Monsieur, breaking all his own rules about gossiping servants, asked Serafin what the Marquis had given the King and how on earth he had managed to have it delivered in such an extraordinary fashion.

"My master is a man of many talents," Serafin said.

"I know that," said Monsieur impatiently. "But this! It was extraordinary! Like magic, almost." Serafin stared at Monsieur.

The man's eyes are really rather odd, thought the nobleman uneasily. They are not the eyes one should see in a servant. Crossly, he blustered, "I am the brother of your master's host and therefore you are to tell me."

Serafin nodded. What was there about that simple, respectful nod that made Monsieur feel both ashamed and angry? Serafin murmured: "Of course, Monsieur. But you must understand that gifts to the King should not be discussed."

Monsieur knew that himself, but he did not care. He surprised himself by pleading. "Please, Serafin. I must know, or those courtiers will make fun of me for not knowing what my guests are doing."

Serafin nodded again, and again Monsieur had a disconcerting glimpse of mockery underneath the politeness. Eventually, Serafin said: "A small portrait, beautifully done, showing an angel against a background of azure sky. Around the portrait a silver frame, the very latest in elegance."

'Is that *all?*"

"The angel had certain features, shall we say. I think the King may have recognized those features."

"You *mean* . . ." Monsieur was flabbergasted by the Marquis's cleverness. Everyone knew that the King's darling at Court was a sweet young woman with a limp and golden hair, a woman who made the poor Queen seem even fatter and plainer than she actually was.

"Yes. Mademoiselle herself."

"Oh, Serafin!" Monsieur so far forgot himself as to slap his thigh in delight. "What a man your master is! It is as if he is guided by an angel himself!"

"I wouldn't go so far as that," Serafin muttered, but Monsieur did not hear her. Flapping his hands vaguely in dismissal, he was off and away toward his daughter's apartment, his legs wanting to break into little jigs now and then. They were set. They were set in the favor of the King now! Hadn't His Majesty said so himself? Ah, even his brother would have to admit Monsieur was a clever operator. After all, it was he who had discovered the Marquis, was it not?

» Sixteen «

Elisabeth and the Marquis walked in the gardens, followed at a respectful distance by Serafin. Monsieur had gone to lie down, quite fatigued by all the excitement and determined to rest before the King's supper, which they must attend. Their guide had sufficiently relaxed to tell them that the King normally ate his dinner alone—that is, with no more than two gentlemen in attendance—but that tonight there was the rare privilege of the King's supper. Of course only the King, his brother, his mother, his wife, and all their family were entitled to seats at the table. The grandest of the courtiers would have stools; the rest had to stand. But anyway, thought the Marquis, he would not be able to eat a thing, so full was he of what had happened that day. And now, walking with his love, Elisabeth, her gloved hand lightly on his arm, he felt so proud that his heart swelled even more.

Elisabeth had heard whispers very quickly of her Marquis's success with the King. Her audience with the Queen had been pleasant but not exciting. Her Majesty seemed like a kind woman, but rather sad, which was not surprising when you considered the stories about the ladies who had a hold of the King's heart. Looking sideways at her suitor, Elisabeth determined that he would never be allowed to do such a thing; she, unlike the poor, sad Queen, would keep her husband's full attention. But anyway, she thought, although she would never have voiced the thought, I am not plain like she is, and such things would never happen. We will live happily ever after. That's the way of it.

As they turned a corner, twittering pleasurably to each other, Serafin a pace behind, they met up with another small party. Elisabeth whispered, "That is the Duke, the King's brother. They do say he . . ." but before she could finish, the others reached them. Smiles, curtsies, bows, exclamations of delight, secret curiosity.

The Duke was a rather short man, with very dark eyes and hair, and a little potbelly swelling under his elaborate clothes. He wore very high-heeled shoes adorned with bows, and his arms and hands were covered in bracelets and rings. The other men with him were also colorfully dressed and ornamented, and their faces wore a look of permanent scorn. But the Duke showed no such scorn.

"Good evening, good evening. Yes, what a hit you made today, my dear Marquis. I must admit I was amazed when I saw the clever gift you had brought. Such a pretty thing, that portrait of Mademoiselle Ange. Ah yes, so clever of you! She has an angelic nature too. Such a sweet thought, so pretty too, with that delicate frame, and how amazing the method of delivery! Truly a clever thought. Especially for a foreigner, I thought. Oh, and Mademoiselle de Saint-Cotin, how are you? I trust your audience with my sister-in-law went well? Yes, yes, a good woman, but a little gloomy you know, my dear. Yes, rather gloomy. Well, I will see you again I am sure, and certainly at Tenebran. I simply *must* see this place. It will be amusing, though I find the provinces fatiguing for any length of time."

He had not stopped to draw breath during this speech, and Elisabeth, who had been told by one of the Queen's ladies-in-waiting what a chatterbox the Duke was, wanted to giggle. The King hardly speaks, the woman had said, but floods pour out of the Duke.

"Your Highness is too good," she said as sweetly as she could. The Duke blinked. "Good? Good? I suppose I am, is that right, gentlemen?"

They agreed with rather supercilious nods. One said, "If by good one means interesting, of course." The Duke laughed. "Of course, of course!"

Just then they were joined by a tall, thin man in priest's clothes. "Monsieur le Marquis," the priest said, in a deep voice. "Allow me to present my congratulations."

"Thank you." The Marquis was not in the least in awe anymore, Elisabeth observed as she watched him talking to the King's chaplain and the Duke and other courtiers who came sauntering up, like bees pretending they did not know there was a honey pot close by. Each of them mouthed pretty words and made pretty gestures of appreciation, and the Marquis and Elisabeth felt they had really fallen among friends.

Alone, unwatched, Serafin stood several paces behind, listening with a heart growing colder and lonelier by the minute. She was sure the Marquis knew it was she who had brought the gift, she who had prevented the King from opening that dangerous box. Yet so far he had said nothing. Perhaps it was because by admitting that he knew he would also be acknowledging that Serafin had powers beyond the ordinary. Or perhaps it was because he had a heart as hollow as a honeycomb, if as sweet.

"It does not seem fair, does it?" The familiar tones made her spin around.

"What are *you* doing here?" she said, without much surprise. Monsieur Balze was dressed more finely than she had previously seen him, in a coat of rich, deep red-brown. His eyes were dancing.

"You had a better gift than me to give. No matter. The box is still with the King."

"It is probably now with one of the courtiers. If the King does not like a gift, he often gives it away to somebody else."

"No matter." He was infuriatingly calm. "What you gave was better. You did not follow the Law there, Serafin. For it mocked the Law, mocked the Queen's sadness in its flaunting of one who is assuredly no angel."

She stared at him. "It was not my choice. It was given to me."

"Ah yes, by your friend in that town, far away. I know him well. Yes."

"He did not choose your way. I know that, or he would not be what he is."

"No. But he knows despair now, because he knows the Law cannot be followed in its entirety."

"It is not up to you to tell me." She turned her back on him, but he stood his ground. After a while, she muttered, "It is not easy, no."

She knew he was smiling broadly without needing to look at him. "Of course it is! Humans are so ungrateful. And so *little*, don't you find? I mean look at them: they think a cat in a silver ribbon is extraordinary, they believe that a fountain is a sign of mastery over nature. What you and I could accomplish, Serafin, beggars their little imaginations. And there would be no need for the loneliness, either. Look at me Serafin . . ."

His voice was low, honeyed, beautiful. She turned her head and saw his eyes, limitless as the deepest pools. Again she saw, beckoning in them, the gifts he would offer: eternal life, worlds without end, the sweetest enchantment. And just for a small price, a small forgetting.

Suddenly, unbidden, without warning, she saw in her mind Frederic standing at the edge of the crowd, speaking for her. She saw the eyes of the others, aglow with casual hate and blood lust. She saw him speaking, and heard his silence too, when it appeared he must break it to stop his banishment. Slowly, without joy, she said, "No. I cannot."

"The Law again," Balze said bitterly. "It will be a cold comfort to you, you will see. You have no more debt to him. You are free. He is now the Marquis. So why stay with him?"

"He still needs me. And I have not completed my task."

Strangely, he smiled, as if the dragging tone of voice pleased him. "You will change your mind. You will see."

» Seventeen «

"Was it not kind of Monsieur Balze to bring Mademoiselle Elisabeth's mirror? She had quite missed it, she said. She does not trust any glass but her own. He really is a very kind man, traveling all that distance for us, don't you think so, Serafin?"

The Marquis patted his hair into shape and winked at himself in the glass. Serafin, watching him, said nothing. The Marquis looked rather put out.

"Oh, Serafin, you are as much fun as a confederation of undertakers at the moment! Cheer up! Life is not all thorns and porridge."

"You are a fool," Serafin said, so suddenly and sharply that the Marquis took a step back. "Don't you see anything? Don't you understand?"

"See? Understand?" The Marquis looked puzzled. "I think you must be very tired, Serafin. You are not making any sense."

Serafin took a step toward him. "Don't you remember who you are? Frederic, the miller's son. That's who. *Frederic, the miller's son.* Shall I say it more loudly?"

"Please, Serafin."

"No more a Marquis than my left arm is! How do you think you came here? Because of your pretty face? Think again, my boy. There are more pretty faces back in your village than there are flowers on a bush, yet do you see them here?"

"But, Serafin . . ."

"No buts. No. Please. I was bound to you by the Law because you opened your stupid mouth and got yourself into trouble on my account, but I am not bound to you for every foolishness. If you do not know what Monsieur Balze means to do, if you do not know who he *is*, you are not only foolish—this

96

I knew long ago—but you are also of an ignorance as criminal as it is stupid. Well. There is not much I can do about that." She turned to go, her hands tingling with the angry sadness.

"Serafin. *Catou.*" His voice was very quiet, no longer affected. "It is hard, you know. If I remember who I am, then I can no longer be the Marquis. And you know I cannot be Frederic, not here. But you . . . you are still you. You have not changed." He swallowed. "I thank you, for the King's gift." He met her eyes, and she clearly saw that he knew what had happened, though he could not voice it. She was surprised to find the softness invading her again. No. She must not. She must be strong.

"I am glad you at least realize that," she said gruffly. "But I do not understand why you must become other in order to live your new life. Not only to pretend, as I do, but to *become.*"

"You change your shape too," he said simply, and she nearly gasped at that, for it showed how far he had come from the village and its fears. *Matagot,* they would have hissed there. Cat-magician, dangerous, unnatural thing. Especially when female. Doubly dangerous, doubly unnatural.

"I . . ." She looked at him, then away.

He said, "Serafin . . . tell me, why do you do this? Why do you give me all this?"

She made an angry gesture, but he kept looking at her, and she felt the uncertain softness rising. "It is the Law," she said stiffly, at last. "The Law, which I must keep to, as I am bound by it."

"Does this Law then make you sad and angry? Is that part of what it must do?" His gaze was open, without anger, but with something she hated to see there—pity.

"Of course not," she almost shouted. "It is *you* who makes me angry. Angry, angry! Never sad. *Never.* You make me angry because you are a blind fool, stumbling on and on with not even a look to see where you are going."

"But I have you," he said gently. "That is what you told me."

There was a knock on the door, and Monsieur's voice called: "Are you ready, Marquis? We should be making our way down."

"Yes, I am coming," answered the Marquis. But instead of immediately leaving, he took a step toward Serafin and hugged her, hard, then released her again. She could not move for surprise, and after he had gone and she was alone, she lifted a hand to her cheeks and found they were wet with tears.

» » « «

"Ah, there is the cat again, Carabas!" Monsieur's voice rang out over the crowd around the supper table. "Better be careful she does not get into a fight with the King's lap dogs," someone said, and someone else called out, "Which ones are those, human or animal?" There was no danger of the King hearing such remarks, for he and his family were at the very front, at the table, and there was such a buzz of conversation as made any monitoring of conversation impossible. Food of various kinds—pastries in cunning shapes, hard-boiled eggs, fruit, and other dainties—was being passed around the crowd, and servants were kept busy hurrying in with more. The black cat weaved in and out of legs, purring, getting a biscuit here, a piece of pastry there.

Getting more to eat than me, thought the Marquis, and sighed. He was finding it difficult to concentrate on the splendor and occasion of this meal. A pulse of something like fear beat under his skin, so that he made lightheaded and not altogether coherent remarks to the lady next to him, who, by misfortune, was not Elisabeth but some raddled old courtier.

His companion did not concern herself about his abstraction. In her circle it was now considered quite the thing to exchange pleasantries with the Marquis of Carabas. And if he was rather quiet at the moment, well, what did it matter? She could construct her own pretty story to delight and divert her friends. She had stood next to the King's latest discovery, she would say, and smile knowingly, and say he was ripe for the taking of any lady with big listening eyes. For to her and her friends, love such as the Marquis and Elisabeth thought they knew was merely a sweet fairy tale to divert children. She did not for a moment suspect that the Marquis would have viewed this attitude with horror and disbelief. She did not notice his desperate glances toward Elisabeth, who stood in her finery like a delicate butterfly among birds of paradise. She did not know that he wished he could just take his love's hand and run away from all this, away into the fields where they would be free. If she had known, she would have clapped her hands and said, "Oh, but how romantic!" and then laughed and batted her eyelashes.

At length the King stood up. Instantly a silence fell on the whole gathering, to be broken by the sound of a single trumpet as the herald announced the King's departure for his bed. As soon as he had gone out of the door with his family, respectfully watched by the crowd, there was a general loosening of the atmosphere.

The Marquis's neighbor said to him, archly, "And now, Sir, we can really have a conversation, and plan our journeys into the unexplored territory of the heart." The Marquis looked at her, then much to her stupefaction, left her there and almost ran toward Elisabeth.

The noblewoman watched him go with astonishment bordering on anger, but this soon changed to malicious enjoyment as she contemplated the story she would have to tell her friends, and how it would reflect so much on the character of the King and his choice of friends.

Part Three

The Lord of Tenebran

» Eighteen «

The cat had picked her delicate way through the feet of the Court, always keeping a wary eye out for the overfed, bad-tempered fluffy dogs beloved of the King. The cat knew that despite the sentimental curiosity about her in the Court, an attack from the dogs would be regarded with amusement by most there, a welcome diversion from the boring routine.

But now that the King had gone, so had the dogs, and the cat had the field to herself. She pressed up against the silk-stockinged legs and rustles of satin and put up bravely with the cooings and strokings of perfumed men and women. She listened to all the whispers and shouts, to the silly ferment of people with too little to occupy them, for people are never afraid to display their basest selves in front of a dumb animal. It was as she was doing her rounds and beginning to feeling rather bilious because of the sugared dainties she had been handed too often, that she heard the word *Tenebran.*

Arching her back, purring prettily, she exited from the lap of a periwigged nobleman and moved quietly in the direction the word had come from. She made herself very small, almost disappearing into the flows and floods of skirts, and listened with every nerve in alert. Strange, to feel frightened in the midst of all this frippery, all these light, bored voices, but suddenly she did, for once again she heard, playing under the others like a bass note, the voice of one she recognized. The Adversary again. Never did this voice raise itself, never did it directly suggest, but somehow it was all the more frightening for that. For the first time, this seemed no longer a contest of wills but something far more dangerous—for the Adversary, unlike her, had no divided nature, and his powers were much greater than hers. And in the faces

of those clustered around her, especially in one, she saw something awaken into full life, something that had probably always
been there but would never have surfaced if not for the urgings
of the voice.

You fools, you fools, the cat would have cried if she could
speak. But she could not—not in this shape—and also she must
not be seen here in this company. Noiselessly, in the invisible way
that only cats have, she melted from the room.

The Marquis, Monsieur, and Elisabeth also left the room
around this time. Monsieur had been surprised to find himself
not as happy in this gathering as he had always imagined he
would be. The world of the Court had gone on without him,
and he could not match wits now with the kinds of people who
mattered. He was annoyed to find himself missing Tenebran and
the peace of its gardens, and astonished to find that in his deepest heart, he was not looking forward anymore to the visit of
the King. Something about the Court, about the people there,
made him feel uneasy, although he would not have said so for a
moment.

As for the Marquis and Elisabeth, well, lovers are never satisfied in a crowd. Younger than Monsieur, they had accepted
much more readily the atmosphere of the Court, but wanted to
be alone for a while. So they had followed Monsieur with some
relief when he had announced he was tired and was turning in.

"Such a splendid evening," Monsieur said brightly as they
left. "But I find I am weary."

"Some very boring people there," remarked the Marquis
without thinking, earning scandalized but assenting glances from
Monsieur and Elisabeth.

She tried to cover for him by saying, even more brightly
than her father: "Mademoiselle Ange spoke very highly of you,
Marquis. Such a lovely lady. So sweet and pleasant, and so *natural.*"

"Hmm," said the Marquis, whose stomach was unpleasantly empty and whose mind was not as easy as he would have
liked it to be.

This reaction pleased his lady, who would have been very upset if he had agreed with her. She gave a little laugh and whispered, "All the same, I am glad not to be at Court all the time."

Both men silently agreed. "My dear children," said Monsieur, "we must be ready to leave by midday tomorrow. Monsieur Balze tells me my brother is rather unwell, and I wish to be back at Tenebran before nightfall."

The two young people looked at him in some dismay. This was the first they had heard of such a thing. Although neither had much feeling for the Lord of Tenebran, especially not the Marquis, who had never even seen his host, it nevertheless cast a pall over them.

Monsieur saw this and smiled. "Do not concern yourself too much," he said. "I am sure my brother will recover. He is often ill."

But when he was back in his room, and the two young people had gone on their way, he allowed himself a brief moment's anxiety for the fate of his brother.

The Marquis and Elisabeth, meanwhile, walked side by side through the great corridors of the palace. They spoke little, for they did not need to. Each knew what the other was thinking, or thought they did. Each took for granted the fact that they would have a long time to know the other, and that matters had been settled for them. The Marquis knew he would never return to his old life; Elisabeth knew that never would she be satisfied with a gilded fool.

At last, they farewelled each other and returned to their separate rooms, there to fall quickly into a dreamless sleep. The Marquis, however, was waylaid by Serafin, who stood in his room as he entered, a complicated look on her face. The Marquis yawned.

"Oh, good night, Serafin. Please, there is no need to wait for me. I will see myself to bed. And I am sure you must be tired yourself. Just . . ."

"Be quiet. Listen to me." Serafin's eyes were blazing. Her white hair, loosened from its daytime bonds, framed her face in an unearthly glow. The Marquis felt a shiver of awe, which he quickly concealed with a grimace of tiredness.

"Must I?" he said plaintively. Serafin did not even bother to answer. She just kept staring at him with those eyes till the Marquis thought he could not bear it.

"There is no time to waste on stupidities. This is what I heard . . . a plot against the King, his son . . . danger." And as she spoke, the Marquis was sure she was growing in stature, her body transforming in front of his dazzled eyes, her white hair glowing more and more. Suddenly, she came to a stop. The Marquis blinked and shook his head, for she was just Serafin: small, tough, angry, uncomfortable. There was no glowing being, no terrifying light. Then he started, for she was glaring at him in an unmistakable manner.

Hurriedly, he said, "Er, that is terrible. Yes. But what can we do, Serafin? Should we go and tell the . . ."

"No." She rapped out the word. She had not told him everything, not told him about the voice underpinning it all. That was not his concern, not a part of his story. But it made her alone with her fear, a fear she desperately tried to suppress.

"So what then should I do?" He looked at her pleadingly. "Serafin, this is too big for me. It frightens me. What on earth can I do?"

"Some things you must decide for yourself." Her lips pursed, her eyes narrowed. "I can't do *everything* for you."

"You already have," he said, dully, and turned away from her. "I am tired, Serafin. Please."

For the first time in their dealings with each other, she hesitated. Then, stiffly, she turned on her heel and walked into her own antechamber. How could she tell him she had no idea herself what to do? How could she say anything about the fear gnawing at her? He would just look at her with his big, soft cow-eyes and weep, probably. Oh, why had she been put in this world at all if it was for such poor creatures? She longed to be like Monsieur Balze: strong, sure of himself, his eyes untroubled by scruples or doubts.

>> >> « «

In the morning they were all of them troubled, out of sorts, and snappy; all except Monsieur Balze, who had emerged bright and early from the stables where he had dossed down for the night. He told them that he had arranged to buy some fresh horses and that the carriage had been polished to within an inch of its life. "I made sure I stood over those lazy servants myself," he said jovially. He did not seem to notice nor care that his lively talk met with little response, except for a few nervous smiles. His eyes often rested thoughtfully on Serafin and the Marquis, but he made no particular remark to them. In fact, none of them had ever seen him so bright and cheerful.

Of course the King would not be farewelling them—they were not important enough. But he had sent his brother, the Duke, to express his pleasure. The Duke was dressed even more fantastically than on the previous day. His shoes were so high that he tottered on them, and the paint and powder on his face were surely a little too thick. But his high, bright voice intoned the ritual words of farewell with just the right amount of plea- sure mixed with mockery, and somehow Serafin felt her spirits rising. The little man's eyes missed nothing; they were dark as currants but shinier, the expression in them both wary and amused. As she watched him, she felt the Marquis's eyes on her and gave a tiny nod: the same thought of telling the Duke about the plot had occurred to them both at the same time. So when the Duke had finished, and Monsieur had made all the ritual an- swers, she took care to walk casually over to Monsieur Balze's side and engage him in conversation while the Marquis bowed over the Duke's hand and thanked him profusely.

"A pity you could not stay here. I wager there is much we could have shown you that you have not yet seen," Serafin heard the Duke say.

"Oh, yes, *such* a pity," the Marquis replied, and Serafin saw Balze's eyes, which had been fixed on them, slide away in bore- dom to her.

"Are you not tired of such painted fools?" Monsieur Balze asked quietly, his lip curled.

"Are *you* not?" she retorted, her heart thudding.

He smiled. "Oh, it is amusing to play with them."

"And for me."

He smiled more broadly. "Come, come, Serafin. You know that is the trouble with your kind: nothing amuses you. Everything is too serious. People get tired of that."

"But I know what is inside your mask," she said, greatly daring. "No amusement there, except for the rictus of a skull."

"Oh, my dear. Fine words. But you know you don't believe them. That is the Law speaking in you, not your true nature. You are not only of the Law, my dear. You are not only of the earth. In you, you combine it all. And don't you know how kin we are?"

Yes, she knew that. Oh yes, she knew that. She snapped, "You may blind and puzzle people with your tricks and your fancies, but you won't do so for me."

He laughed softly. "Look all around you, my dear. What do you think has the greatest following—your Law or my freedom? How long do you think you can stand against it? Why, your little pets, your funny little people whom you guard so closely: you will see, they will choose my freedom rather than your rules. That is the way it has always been. My freedom is the king of the world."

"Then why are you always here, trying to force your *freedom* on these funny little people, as you call them? If you are king of the world, why be forced to live like a servant?" She could see the Duke listening to the Marquis, his mobile face suddenly still so that his resemblance to his brother was quite plain, and her spirits rose again.

Balze saw her glance, looked in his turn but not for long. "You see that man, for instance. What do you think it matters to him, your stupid Law? He breaks it every day, gladly, without even knowing he is doing so. He is constantly with those who would laugh even at the mention of such things. And he is not alone."

"What do you know?" She shrugged, though her heart beat faster with her fear. He made no answer, but looked at her with laughing eyes, eyes that saw into nearly every corner of her.

107

"Oh, I know. It is my business to know."

"You did not answer my question." She could see the Duke leaving now, making extravagant bows and the others returning them. She looked fully at Balze. "Why, if you're the king, do you have to dress as a servant? Is it because you must cheat and lie and deceive in order to gain your ascendancy, because in your true shape all would turn from you in horror? Is it because you will do anything, anything, to fill your eternal emptiness, even as you destroy those 'little people' you're so contemptuous of?"

"Here is a question of my own," he said, his eyes darkening. "Why are *you* not in your true shape? Why do *you* hide and pretend? Why do you choose to use your powers to unworthy ends? Shape-shifting as a cat—pah! Helping ill-mannered, stupid village folk go higher than they imagine or deserve—pah! Never questioning anything, repeating: 'It is the Law, it is the Law!' Pah, and pah again!"

She did not answer him. It did not seem important anymore, and anyway, she was afraid she would have no answers.

» Nineteen «

It was a silent party that made its way back down the country roads to Tenebran. Monsieur Balze had declared that he still had some business to transact and would meet them afterward, and no one had challenged him. It was almost as if he were the master now, not Monsieur, who simply nodded wearily when the steward spoke.

Serafin, sitting up with the driver, noted with a heart getting heavier and heavier how the countryside seemed emptier and emptier of life the closer they came to Tenebran. The village where they had stopped so happily on the way to the palace was quite deserted when they passed through, and from then on there were only empty fields, turning eventually into the bleak rock-strewn hillsides and flatlands around Tenebran. The driver, his hands expertly on the horses' reins, mumbled, "Back home we go, oh ho!"

"You love your home, do you?" said Serafin, looking with sorrow at the desolation around her.

The man laughed bitterly. "Love it! I have forgotten it. My home used to be there. See, beyond the hill. When the ogre— beg pardon—when the Lord of Tenebran came, we were part of a village. Yes, three villages in fact, none of them called Tenebran. They came and they razed the houses and they poisoned the land, for the Lord wanted no habitation near his castle. Then the best part they built on and planted gardens, and then they offered some of us jobs. Only the young ones, mind. The old ones were driven off, given as they were of no use any longer."

She looked at him. He did not seem perturbed, his hands still light on the reins. He went on: "Some fools have come back. They try to grow food there in that blighted land. Fools!"

She did not make any response to this, her mind on the next part of the fate she must fulfill. She said sternly, "Stop the horses!" And as the startled man obeyed, she jumped down from her seat, heading off toward some people she could see working hopelessly and backbreakingly among the rocks.

She heard the shouts behind her, but did not stop. Her mind burning, she walked rapidly and did not stop till she had reached the people, who stood watching her approach. They were the most ragged and wretched people she had ever seen. Their eyes were not completely defeated, but there was no welcome in them. Instead, they were full of a dull fear and distrust.

"Good people, to whom do these lands belong?" she asked, her voice hoarse and strange.

The people exchanged frightened glances, clutching a little at one another. Finally someone was thrust forward and mumbled, "Please, Sir, we did not mean . . ." We know that all these lands hereabouts belong to the Lord of Tenebran, but we thought that perhaps he would not mind if . . ."

"They belong to the Marquis of Carabas!" Serafin said in ringing tones. "Do you hear me? They belong to the Marquis of Carabas. If anyone asks you, that is what you must answer." She looked defiantly at them, breathing hard, and saw their faces close over, their eyes go dead. Suddenly, there were tears on her cheeks again, scalding, and her mouth opened without her having planned it, and she heard herself say: "And the Marquis of Carabas believes that every peasant must have his own land, and to each shall be given according to his needs. To each shall be given a plot of land and he shall be free as long as he lives and his sons and daughters after him." She knew that what she had just said was not in the Law, not in the words she knew she had to say, and she was aghast at the silence that fell then. For a moment their faces remained stiff with dread, then all at once something in them dissolved and she felt rather than heard their gabble, their excitement. And then she heard behind her the voices of those she had left in the carriage. But she did not say a word to them. She did not say a word to anybody, just turned in the other direction, toward Tenebran, leaving all the chatter and astonishment and joy behind her.

She was alone now, she thought as she ran: not in the Law, not completely human either, a speck trying to stop the machinery moving, keep the wheels of justice turning. She had gone beyond the role allotted to her into a space that was still uncharted. And yet she must go to the end, for now she thought she saw the darkness of the future ahead of her.

As she ran, she thought she felt the landscape around her changing, so that rocks turned into houses and the hills softened their shapes and became clothed in green and the fields became full of crops. She could smell the scent of new-mown hay and see the teams of workers tying and sheaving, their voices ringing out with song, the songs of the free. And she thought of how she had gone beyond the Law and changed things forever, and was then both afraid and elated. She had decided on something for herself; she had gone beyond her destiny and had changed the enchantment.

She ran and ran till the breath was ragged and rough in her lungs, and soon she was at the gates of Tenebran. She ran into the grounds and was amazed to see how nothing had changed there. Everything was as beautiful as ever, yet with a strangely seedy quality, as if at any moment it might all crumble to dust. She thought of Monsieur Balze, riding urgently on his swift horse and thought: I must hurry, I must hurry, there can be no time to lose now. Her feet flew on the graveled walks, past the completed theatre for the King, through the grotto, past the lake with its swans as ornamental as statues, up the terrace and its stairs, through the reception rooms, and up the marble staircase.

At last she reached the room where she had met the Lord of Tenebran. She slowed, and was utterly silent, listening, hearing nothing, not a breath, not a sign of life. Fear thudded through her again, for she had stepped outside the rules now and did not know where any of it would take her. She took a step forward and pushed noiselessly at the door. It opened easily as before, and she was inside the shadows of the room again.

For a moment she could see nothing; the room was even darker than the last time. She took another step and heard the door click behind her, with a sound of utter finality. And then she heard the voice: "What took you so long? Come, come so I may see you for what you are."

» Twenty «

Monsieur had been dozing quietly in a corner of the carriage when it suddenly stopped. He was wrenched from a most pleasant dream and came to in a mumble of discomfort. His daughter and the Marquis also seemed disagreeably surprised by the sudden stop, though Monsieur saw with tenderness that in their case they had not been distracted from sleep but from a prolonged bout of hand-holding and eye-gazing. The Marquis stuck his head out of the window and called out, "Hey! What is happening?" before turning to Monsieur and Elisabeth and saying rapidly, "It's Serafin. I'm not sure what is going on, but I think I had better go and find out." For a moment Monsieur felt seriously annoyed: what was wrong with all these servants, that they should so overstep their place? Then, as both the Marquis and Elisabeth left the carriage and hurried over the fields to where they could see Serafin talking with some peasants, he decided he really must go and find out himself. After all, he was the closest relative of the Lord of Tenebran, wasn't he?

But none of them were used to walking in plowed fields with high-heeled shoes, and by the time they had stumbled over to the group, Serafin had already gone. They could only just see the slight figure running, running toward the castle, whose roofs shimmered in the near distance. But somehow that shimmer seemed less real than the soft glow of the crops—the splendor of Tenebran a distant echo of the natural splendor of field and sky. The peasants did not watch them coming; they had returned to working, their scythes working rhythmically.

Monsieur stopped. He rubbed his eyes and yawned. "I could have sworn . . ." he muttered. Then he rubbed his eyes again. "But no matter." The Marquis and Elisabeth said nothing, but their hands crept out toward each other. Monsieur watched them with a heart suddenly light as a bird. "Do you know, I have never come into the fields before? I have always thought that the countryside hereabouts was bleak and ugly. But now I see I was wrong." Now I see my brother is not the tyrant I half-feared he was, he thought. Look at these people here: well fed, their very movements denoting happiness. "Good people," he called out merrily. "Do you give thanks to your lord?"

The peasants did not pause in their work, but one called back: "Ah yes. But that is because our lord does not curb our freedom."

"You see." Monsieur turned smilingly to the other two, who did not see at all but nodded anyway. "Good people," he called out again. "What do you do for your lord?"

This time the man who had spoken earlier put down his scythe and said, "We give of our own free will, not because of any binding."

"You see," repeated Monsieur, who did not see himself at all that time. The Marquis and Elisabeth, hands tightly clasped, made no answer. Then Monsieur walked in his tight shoes closer to the peasants and said, "So the rule of the Lord of Tenebran is light?"

There was a silence. The spokesman glanced back at the other workers. His face closed, as did theirs, but he said nothing. And then a little voice called out: "Our lord is not the Lord of Tenebran. It is the Marquis of Carabas."

If he had picked up a thunderbolt and flung it, it would not have created a bigger shock. Monsieur went quite pale, as did the Marquis and Elisabeth. The peasants were completely silent. Then Monsieur spoke, in a voice quite unlike his normal light tones. "Who has told you that?"

"It is the truth," said the little voice, with a kind of laugh to it. Try as Monsieur might to identify it, he could not, yet somehow it convinced him. He said again very quietly, "Who has told you that?"

At last the spokesman said, "It is the truth, Sir. Our hearts have told us so."

"Your hearts?" Monsieur stared at him.

"A man, dressed all in brown," said the little voice insistently, coldly. "He told us. It was his master bade him tell us so."

"Why?" Monsieur turned to the Marquis. "Surely you did not . . ."

The Marquis was still as pale as his own shirt. He gazed at Monsieur. He opened his mouth, but no sound came out. Elisabeth had withdrawn her hand from his, and his palm where her hand had so lightly rested felt icy cold without it.

"Have we not treated you well enough?" Monsieur said sorrowfully. "Or are things different in Spain—do guests repay their host in such a fashion?"

"Father . . ." began Elisabeth, but the little voice piped up again, mockingly: "The Marquis of Carabas is a real man. He understands us." Still Monsieur could not see the person who had spoken, but his voice seemed to penetrate Monsieur's skull with a piercing clarity.

Monsieur could not say anything; his throat was tight with tears. But his gaze at the Marquis was full of reproach, so blinded by it that he did not see the awakening sorrow in the Marquis's eyes, or the grief in his daughter's. He said heavily, at last: "We had better get back to the castle. I will have to tell my brother of this, of course. Though if he is unwell, I do not wish to make him any worse. Come, Elisabeth. I think the Marquis can find his own way to Tenebran."

It did not occur to him that the Marquis might choose not to go back to Tenebran. Indeed he was right not to think so, for the possibility did not occur to the Marquis either. The latter just stood there and watched as his love and her father moved slowly back to the carriage, feeling as if his whole life were draining away into the rich soil under his feet. He did not see or notice the peasants getting back to work. He did not wonder at their capacity to do so even after such events, for he knew that the work of making food counted for much more than anything else in their lives. Lords might come and lords might go, but the work of crops was everlasting. He knew that because of who he was, who he had been, though he had done his best to forget. Eventually he roused himself enough to start walking slowly back to the distant castle, his heart heavier even than the mud on his fine shoes, the spell he had been under dropping from him by the second. He was alone now, afraid, but he must go back to the castle, he knew that in his heart.

>> >> « «

Meanwhile, Monsieur's head was a whirl of thoughts, none of them pleasant. He felt a hot, confused headache coming on. If he did mention this to his brother, the Marquis would be turned out of Tenebran. At the very least, his daughter's heart would be broken, and his own trust in humanity destroyed. But if he did not, there would be no retribution for what was at the very least a most discourteous act—and an act not easy to unbind, for a quarrel between nobles must not involve peasants.

He could not understand at all why the Marquis should have done such a thing. Had he been completely mistaken in the young man? Was he truly an adventurer without scruple, even if undoubtedly also a great nobleman? The success of the young man at the court of the Sun King had impressed him greatly, but now that the doubts had been planted, Monsieur found himself reviewing everything about the Marquis: the way they had met, the way he had acted since then, his behavior at Court, and the cat. And that strange servant of his. Unease and dismay frothed in him, making him feel quite ill, as did the unaccustomed feel of having to make a decision. And a look at his daughter's sad face made him feel worse. Suddenly he could not bear it any longer. He reached forward and patted Elisabeth's hand.

"You could not know. Do not grieve, my dear," he said gently.

It was then that he received the second shock of the day, for Elisabeth withdrew her hand and burst out with: "What do you know? Why does it take only one voice to immediately condemn someone you have liked up till now? Why didn't you give him a chance to explain himself?"

His pretty, gentle daughter was red as a beetroot, her chest heaving, her eyes flashing contempt. Monsieur felt as if she had slapped him. He stammered, "But what reason could there be? Is it not at the very least a gross impoliteness, at the most a terrible treason to covet your host's land?"

"Who said that was what he had done? Just that little peasant. And you believed a stranger rather than your own heart."

She looks so like her mother when her temper is up, he thought suddenly, and the grief he had pushed away for so long came flooding back. "My dear Elisabeth, you know I desire only your happiness. And I know that you and the Marquis love each other, just as I loved your mother dearly. But loyalty is also important, and I must be loyal to my brother." He shook his head, for the headache was getting worse; his forehead felt clamped by an iron band.

"Loyal to *him?* Why, Father? You know that he cares not a whit about us or anyone else. We are there at his castle merely to be witnesses to his splendor—a splendor he does not even enjoy. Sometimes I wonder if he even really exists, if he has a soul at all."

"Elisabeth! My brother helped us when we were in great need. It may not seem important to you, and the world could be well lost for love, but I can assure you that poverty is not an ennobler of souls."

Her chin jutted out. "I do not care. I *know* what matters, and we must follow our hearts. Did you know, Father, that your brother is known as the ogre hereabouts?"

"That is a dreadful slander." His voice was tired. "Just because he is rich and powerful, people envy him."

"No, Father." This time her voice was softer, her eyes full of pity. "It is because of what he has done. Ask yourself why those people out there were happy to claim the Marquis as their lord. Your brother, and his steward, have shown neither love nor pity, or even the barest attention to the wretched. You know very well how that countryside looked even yesterday. Oh, Father, open your eyes!"

His heart was thudding, his palms were sticky and tingling, but Monsieur still said, his voice remote and sad: "It is all as may be. But what gives the Marquis the right to do what he did? And what gives you the knowledge that he would be any better than my brother? I have not heard him expound on the miseries of the people, and on his determination to right them!"

"What did Carabas *do*?" Elisabeth shot back. "Tell me. What he has done is to make my world real. What he has done is to bring joy and laughter to our lives. He does not need to expound on anything: the way he *is* is what matters."

"Why then didn't you stay with him? Why aren't you out there walking with him?" For the first time, Monsieur's voice hardened.

Elisabeth looked at him and lowered her eyes. "Yes," she said at last. "I was foolish not to. But Father, I suppose I am loyal too: to you."

Monsieur's eyes moistened at that, but he did not weep as he would have done only a few short days before. "Oh, Elisabeth, my dear daughter," he said. And then, after a while, "But what are we going to do? Oh, Elisabeth, *what* are we going to do?"

» Twenty-One «

There he was: the ogre, the Lord of Tenebran, his massive frame slumped in his chair, his blind eyes searching. Serafin stood there without moving, every nerve in her body tingling with fear. The ogre's voice was soft and without emphasis, but somehow it was more frightening than the first time, when a raw energy had seized it.

"I knew you would be back. I know what you have done."

"It is easy to talk," said Serafin, trying to keep her voice steady. "If you know all that, you know also that your end has come."

The ogre laughed, a thin laugh that hardly touched his big body. "Little flea, little cat," he said, mockingly. "You think such as you can defeat *me*? I, who have done things such as you would not dream of in your wildest fantasies! Why, I have such powers at my command as you can only dream of!"

"I have greater ones," said Serafin. "Because they are truly mine to command, whereas yours are not. You are a puppet."

The ogre laughed again. "Puny powers! Do you think I have not heard of your exploits at Court? Do you think such things mean anything against what I can do? Come closer, little flea. Your presumption amuses me. I could, of course, destroy you in one second. Watch!"

And suddenly where there had been a slumped body was a massive presence, bright as the sun, eyes as hot as the fires of the earth: a huge lion, roaring mightily, its mane strangely reminiscent of the ogre's hair. Its feral smell filled the room so that Serafin almost choked. But she stood her ground, even as the lion approached her, roaring horribly, one massive paw upraised.

"I am not afraid of you," she panted, though her heart beat so fast she felt as though it would burst out of her chest. "Get back from me. You know you cannot touch me. You are merely an instrument, a burnt-out husk of humanity too long in thrall to evil. Is that all you can do? Any little power can turn itself into a *lion*. It takes far more courage and intelligence to be a mere cat, as you put it."

The lion flashed and disappeared. In its place was the ogre again, standing this time, staggering a little, as if the effort of transformation had dealt him a blow.

"See?" said Serafin. "You are a mere shell. You are no longer even human. You are a discarded nothing—the Adversary's plaything, broken."

"I am much *more* than human," said the ogre in a loud voice. "All fear me. All envy me. I will live forever. My name shall never die."

"Is that what he promised you? Poor fool, and you believed him. Look at yourself, oh Lord of Tenebran. Come closer. Come to me. Look in my eyes and see what he has made of you—a living death."

"No!" the ogre shouted. "Look at *me!*" And in an instant he disappeared, and in his place was a rat, with red eyes and long teeth, whose breath stank even worse than the lion's. Its eyes glowed like coals, its scream of defiance was terrifying. But instead of Serafin, there was now a cat, an ordinary black cat, but with blazing eyes and a ruff of white around its neck that shone like a moon through the gloom. The cat and rat faced each other. A long hissing breath came from the rat, and in its terrible eyes, the cat saw things that nearly made it falter: a hatred as long and desolating and cold as the universe, as without pity or reason or pain as the remotest burning star. Suddenly the rat lunged, but the cat, with a blinding motion, had it spread eagled under claws more terrible than they had seemed, claws steel-tipped and heavy as lead. The rat's red eyes flashed, it fought desperately, but it was no use—the cat had it firmly pinned down. At that moment another voice came from the gloom.

"Kill it, kill it, it's half-dead already." The voice was light, amused. Its owner presently strolled out of the shadows, hair perfectly in place, eyes full of knowing laughter.

The cat's muscles gathered, but then relaxed. Its lamp-bright eyes stared at the newcomer, and for a moment it made no move. Then very slowly, as if reluctantly, it relaxed its grip completely. The rat just lay there for a second or two, and then its outlines began to blur, its hideous shape changing until it had resolved into a big, spent human body lying on the floor.

The newcomer paid no attention at all to it. Instead, he watched with amusement as the cat slowly and tiredly changed back into Serafin.

"Nearly caught you that time, didn't we?" Monsieur Balze was not at all put out. "And with a mere instrument, a mere discarded human! You really *wanted* to kill him, didn't you? You really hated him, didn't you?"

Serafin said nothing. There was a sickening ache in the deepest part of her being. All at once she knew that what she had seen in the rat's eyes had been a reflection of her own eyes. As the rat had lain there, so ugly and vicious and helpless under her paws, she had known a joy that sang through her veins, a joy that came of great power and vengeance and *rightness*.

"You have broken the Law now, you know that, in letting the evildoer live." Monsieur Balze smiled. "That thing there has killed people without mercy, looted without compunction, sold its soul without a qualm. 'Vengeance is mine,' the Law says. Your ancestors would not have hesitated for one minute, for one second. That is how far you have fallen."

Serafin raised her head and looked at him. In that room, in that hopelessness, he alone was beautiful and perfect, radiating utter confidence. The ache throbbed in her—the pain, the knowledge that she had failed. She should have destroyed the thing that lay on the floor, the unnatural horror of it. That had been her destiny, as it had been Frederic's to be guided by her. It was true. She had broken the Law, and now she was outcast even from her own kind, whose only saving grace had been to

121

mold the destiny of men so that they would know and follow the Law.

"But the Law was made to be broken," went on Balze, coming closer to Serafin. "That is because it is bad law. It does not take account of the nature of humans, and in its own rightness and rigidity, it does more evil than any freedom ever did. Serafin . . . you and I, we are alike too, you know. We are *kin*. You know that, don't you? You have always known that. Your ancestors were my brothers long ago. I understood that the Law was wrong, and they followed me for a while before becoming overcome by fear again. Once they were princes, like me; they had everlasting power like me. But they lost their fine beauty and chose to mate with humans. And so they chose to die. While I . . . I live forever! Take my path, Serafin. You have no choice now, you see."

On the floor the ogre stirred a little. Blinded eyes opened a slit, muscles twitched. But neither Serafin nor Balze took any notice.

"You have no choice," went on the steward, "because now you have broken the Law, you have no home: not with your ancestors the angels, not with humans. You will wander eternally, forever an alien to all worlds. But if you come with me, you will have a destiny rich and rare. Kings and emperors will call you friend. The most beautiful men and women will bless your name. Come, come, Serafin, you know who I am. I am the Adversary, the Brightest Angel. You know that I give all to all who are with me."

Slowly, through parched lips, Serafin said, "Is that why the Lord of Tenebran lies on the floor, a broken shell?"

"The Lord of Tenebran!" Balze laughed. "That is no lord!" He kicked at the supine body. "That is, as you say, merely a shell. *I* am the true Lord of Tenebran, the Lord of Darkness, the Lord of the World." His presence, hot and fragrant as fire, flamed in the room; his beauty and power were awesome. "Come with me, and I will make you my duke, my general."

"But the Marquis . . . and the others . . . Why me? Why do you need me?" Serafin's throat hurt, and the words came slower and slower, for she did not know any longer why she spoke, why she resisted at all.

Balze shrugged. "You know *why*. Because you are my kin, of the greatest kin of all—the Firstborn, the ones of the Law. Those humans? They have mere human lives, unimportant. The things they want and cherish are so unimportant, worthless. In a few short years they will be dead, and what does that matter? If they had never lived, nobody would be any the poorer for it, not even themselves. Somebody else would have been born in their place. Human beings are worth no more than blades of grass, you know that, Serafin: up today, gone tomorrow, things that rot and burn. If you give up that part of your nature, if you come with me, then you will live forever, and all will fear you and envy you."

"Is that why there were also no blades of grass around Tenebran?" Serafin spoke in a whisper.

"Blades of grass?" Balze looked impatient. "A mere image. Do not waste time on such things when your destiny is at stake."

But Serafin's mind had suddenly called up the memory of the way the countryside had changed as she ran toward Tenebran. All at once her nostrils filled with the sweet, dry smell of hay, and her skin tingled with the feel of the swishing grass. She murmured, "If the Law had indeed been against me, would that have been so?"

Balze frowned for the first time. "It is no use buying time now. You have come to the end, and you must make your decision. It is *I* who have the power, I who have all knowledge."

But Serafin was not listening. She was remembering the village, and harvesttime there. She saw her mother preparing food like everyone else, and her heart swelled with sadness for that lost time, that lost childhood in which she had known none of this, or at least only a very little. She had known she was different from the others, but she had still run in the grass and climbed trees and caught tadpoles like the other children. And so had Frederic. Before she could stop herself, before she could really think, she said: "I have made my decision, Balze. I will not come with you."

The look he turned on her then was one such as she had never dreamt in her worst nightmare. For his bright, cold, empty eyes were suddenly the eyes of the abyss, the terrible hunger of nothingness, the thing that was more devouring even than hatred: the face of pure evil. Then he caught himself and laughed. "You will regret this. Like the humans, you are dust, a mere nothing that I will crumble up in my hand, just like that!"

He moved swiftly over to where the ogre was now beginning to sit up. His mocking smile changed into one of commiseration as he helped the stumbling figure up. With a shock, Serafin saw clearly at last that the ogre was old; older than old, his face a blank mask of time. What had once been lively was now so distant as to be almost gone completely. Horror and a painful pity filled her.

"My Lord of Tenebran," said Balze softly, "we have traitors in our midst." And as he spoke, Serafin realized that now was indeed an end. She thought of what the young man had said to her in that town on a night that seemed so long ago: "Do not discount the things you may think most humble. They may save you all in the end." Yes, and so the thought of grass had saved her from being devoured by the great hunger of the abyss, the hunger of the Adversary, but it had not saved them all in the end. Her kind were indeed cursed with incomplete knowledge. And there was nothing now that she could do about it.

» Twenty-Two «

The Marquis of Carabas finally reached the gates of the castle. He had long ago taken off his shoes, and his stockings had torn underfoot, leaving his feet to be splashed by mud and cut by thorns and stones as he made his way through a countryside that he did not even see. Nor did he see the way people stopped working as he passed and watched him go with pity and sympathy, for they knew he was on his way to meet the ogre. As he entered the grounds, however, he saw there were cracks in the hitherto smooth paving, that several of the statues appeared to have toppled over, and that grass was growing over what had been, surely, the brand-new theatre for the King. Dark stains had appeared on the beautiful pale walls, and the silver-tiled roofs were discolored. It was a horrible sight—as if a hundred years or more had passed and he was witnessing the destruction of a great house. Perhaps that was indeed the case? He did not know anymore what could be discounted. Since he had left the village, everything imaginable and not had happened to him: why then might a hundred years not have passed? *He* did not seem to have aged, but then that was probably just a part of the spell. At that thought, fear seized him, and he almost turned his back on that place and ran away. But then the image of Elisabeth came into his mind, and he groaned and dragged his steps closer to whatever lay waiting for him inside.

He came up the great steps and through the terrace, noticing as he did so the rank air of neglect in the gardens and the way spiders and all kinds of other creatures scuttled out of his way as he approached. This was no longer a rich and pleasant enchantment: it was a nightmare, but he must see it through to the end. He knew now why the name *Tenebran* had been familiar to him. It was not only because of Balze, but because the word was close to *darkness*. Spoken differently it could sound light, bright, beautiful, but now it loomed like darkness in his mind, the destruction of all his hopes, the triumph of evil.

Nobody was about in the rooms of the castle: not a servant, not another living creature. Yet there was a presence, a waiting, that rustled all around him. Something whispered in his mind—something that drew him on and on, past the rooms where he had been so happy, past the reception rooms and up the marble staircase, up into what he now saw was the center of the castle. The corridor on the left was a direct artery to the heart of Tenebran, and not some forgotten byway. He had never been there before, and yet his steps unhesitatingly took him on. At length they stopped outside a closed door, which opened easily when he pushed at it.

"We have been expecting you." The room was quite light, although all the curtains were drawn, and the Marquis blinked a little at the brightness. Somehow he was not at all surprised to see that it was Monsieur Balze who had spoken, just as he was not surprised to see Serafin there. And the other figure, the one in the chair—something very like it had been at the edges of his thoughts in his painful walk back to Tenebran.

"I wonder that you show your face here." The voice from that figure was thin, much lighter than he had expected, and he stood blinking in some surprise, trying to clear his gaze of the harsh light so that he could see the ogre better. At last he found his voice. "My Lord, I did no harm. I did not . . ."

"You will speak when I say so." The voice was growing a little louder now, more colored—and the color was anger. Serafin said nothing at all, did not even look at him. Had she, too, deserted him?

At that moment the door was pushed open violently again, and there stood Elisabeth, and behind her, trying to hold her back, Monsieur. "I tell you, it's no use, come back here!" he was shouting in a most unaristocratic kind of way. Then he fell silent as he took in the sight of them all. Monsieur Balze walked to them both and mockingly bowed. "Come in, come in. Come and watch the sport!" he said, and his eyes glittered with joy.

Elisabeth came with not a glance at him, and then walked straight to the Marquis. She flinched a little at the sight of the ogre, but otherwise kept her composure. Monsieur followed much more reluctantly, with sideways glances here and there. But then he stopped short for he had caught a real sight of the figure in his chair. He gave a little cry. "Oh brother, my poor brother! What has happened to you? What have they done to you?"

The ogre turned his blank mask of a face toward Monsieur, but the eyes gave no sign of having really seen him. Instead, he said, "You talk too much. Be quiet."

Monsieur whispered, "But oh, my brother! You look so ill. Why didn't you tell me before. I could have . . ."

"Silence!" roared the ogre. "You did not know or care. As long as *you* had all you needed, what did you care what unspeakable things kept you here? You closed your eyes and your ears. And now you have been harboring a traitor, who seeks to become the Lord of Tenebran in my stead!"

"I did not know," Monsieur whispered. "Truly I did not. None of us did."

"Then you were fools," said the ogre. He turned his stiff, crumbling head to the steward. If I did not have Monsieur Balze here, I would now be lying dead on the ground, and all my power gone.

Elisabeth said then, her eyes blazing, "You condemn the Marquis without even hearing a word from his mouth!" She turned fully to face the ogre, with hardly a quiver. "You are cowards, all of you."

The ogre turned his sightless eyes toward her, and the depth of coldness in those blank pupils made her feel as if an icy hand were clutching at her throat. "It was I who gave you everything," the ogre's voice said. "Even the pretty thoughts in your empty head. And you are not even grateful. Not even a dog's gratitude do I have."

Elisabeth's eyes watered, but she stood her ground. "You gave me nothing worth having!" she said, tossing her head. The ogre laughed then, a terrible sound without any mirth at all.

"I could give you *nothing* with a flick of the fingers," he said. "Then you would find out if it was worth having, my dear little girl!"

Monsieur Balze said smoothly, reassuringly, "I am sure, my Lord, that Mademoiselle did not mean much by her words." And he bowed toward Elisabeth. But somehow the servile gesture, contrasted with the mocking look in his eyes, made her more frightened than anything the ogre had said or done so far. And then the Marquis moved toward her, as if coming out of a spell, and touched her hand. Immediately their fingers interlaced, the warm skin and hard bone almost woven together, a comforting reality in that nightmare. The others watched them, not moving.

"You are right, Balze," the ogre said. "Their words mean very little."

Monsieur took a step toward the ogre, opened his mouth, but no words came out. Balze said, looking attentively at his nails, "Perhaps, my Lord, the fault lies not with master but with servant. After all, it was Serafin, was it not, who spoke to the peasants in the field? It is Serafin, my Lord, who has been creeping in and out, Serafin who is the accursed *matagot*. So it cannot reasonably be said that it is the Marquis behind this, but Serafin: Serafin who has come from who knows where, Serafin with powers of darkness. Why turn into a cat? Why, everyone knows that a cat is an alien, a creature of the unknown, of night! And perhaps the hate of others is well founded."

His words were not directed at the ogre anymore, but at the Marquis, who stood with unblinking gaze, his fingers clasped in Elisabeth's, his feet bleeding and muddy. Now he turned that gaze on Serafin, who stood in silence as she had from the first moment the others had come into the room.

"Do you want to know who Serafin *really* is?" Balze said, pressing closer, as if sensing an advantage. "Do you want to find out what lies behind Serafin's words and actions, what hand is moving the strings? Listen closely, then. A long time ago, long before time was even recorded, there was the Law. And the Law brought into existence everything on Earth and beyond it, and created creatures of the air and of the sea, of the night and of day, of Earth and of eternal life. There were those princes of the air and of the sunrise, the sons of the Law, the angels of light, who one day came together and saw that although the Law had created them, it had come to an end, and its creatures were now free. And so some of them unbound themselves from the Law and became free. But some could not cope with their freedom and became afraid, and in their fear they tried to make their peace with the Law. But you see the Law does not allow for return or remorse, for the Law knows only fierce workings. When those fallen angels saw that, they went to Earth, where they mated with women and lived with fear all their lives. And it is that fear that created evil and pain in the world; it is through the union of those fallen angels and humans that evil came into life. For they are neither angel nor human, but something unnatural and uncreated and unfree—bound by the Law but not recognized by it. Serafin is one of those beings, a descendant of that cursed race who have brought evil and pain and unhappiness to the world. They are alien to this world and should never have been in it. Look at it, at this being, all of you."

They looked at her, and in that blazing light, she seemed both smaller and uglier than they had ever realized. Her white hair did not glow, but clung like dirty ashes to her head. Her eyes were dulled, yet seemed filled with an emotion they could not place, something cold and strange. Monsieur began, "There is something . . ." when the Marquis interrupted him. His voice seemed to have taken on an odd accent, almost like that of the peasants. He said slowly, drawing each word out: "But you said only some of the rebel angels came to Earth. What happened to the other angels, those who had unbound themselves?"

Balze gave a little nod, almost as if he were surprised. "A good question, my dear Marquis. It is good to cover all the ground, is it not? The other princes of the air stayed free. They

129

had no need of the Law, and they knew no death. They had no need for men's affairs, but occasionally helped them when it was necessary. There was one especially—a leader among them, a king of the air, yet who bound himself to men's needs when they desired it. He was the Bright One." He smiled modestly.

"I see," said the Marquis, sounding more countrified than ever and nodding, too. "That is good to know."

Balze looked at him with a little smile, then said: "Now, we are all reasonable. I am sure this problem can be sorted out. All it requires is for the truth to be told and proper judgments to be made." And he smiled again at the Marquis, and in his eyes the latter saw the promise of a new life: more happiness than he could have contemplated, more riches and splendor too, and back, far back in the eyes, the promise that *he* would be the new Lord of Tenebran, that the ogre's reign was finished. All this the Marquis saw and more, but he said nothing.

The ogre waved a hand. "To judgment then," he said impatiently.

"Yes, my Lord," said Balze mock-humbly. "It will be done. It will be swift. Come here, Serafin."

And to the astonishment of all, Serafin came toward him.

» Twenty-Three «

The King considered that the news the Marquis of Carabas had given him merited at least an extra parcel of nobility. His brother, the Duke of Orleans, had lost no time in conveying the news to him, and he swiftly had the plotters brought before him. Their talk of poisoning his son had been idle, but he nevertheless decided it was serious enough to warrant strong action. They were whipped, stripped of title and land, and banished. The King of France was not one to respond overmuch to talk of clemency, and he had refused to believe their pleas that the idea had been planted in their heads, though he believed in strange powers himself. Now, he decided, the Marquis would become the lord of his own substantial holding, lately owned by the plotters.

He would announce this to the Marquis when he went to Tenebran. It would be a wonderful surprise, one worthy of the greatest king in the world.

» » « «

In the ogre's room, Balze was putting forward the case against Serafin. He wove it very cleverly, not mentioning at all the fact that the Marquis had once been a miller's youngest son, but instead presenting the whole thing as the evil concoction of a cursed being.

In all his subtlety, he knew that to tell the truth, however damaging, would make the whole thing appear stupid, a hoax perpetrated on the vain and the foolish and the gullible. There was not a voice raised in the room besides his own as he spoke, and Serafin seemed to shrink further and further as Balze gained in stature and beauty and light. Then at last he stopped, and said, "Have you anything to say in your defense?"

Serafin said nothing at all. Despair had invaded her completely, and she was just waiting for an end to be made of it all. She could see it all now. The destiny of her and her kind was to be the explanation for all the world's ills. The highest Law had abandoned her; the human world with its half-Law had never seen her as part of its own. Oh, the Marquis would flourish as the Lord of Tenebran after a suitable period. The real hunger of the Adversary, the being who called himself Balze, would be salved for a while, till the Marquis was himself sucked dry and another was needed to feed on, for the Lord of Darkness cannot exist without human hosts. Monsieur and Elisabeth would be kept in the style to which they had become more than accustomed. They might be made a little uncomfortable for a little while, but they would forget. The ogre would be completely absorbed into the yawning abyss that was Balze, and would be forgotten too. In time the countryside would become bleak and rocky again, all life leached out of it. But that was human nature. That was it.

"Nothing, then?" said Balze. His eyes shone. "Then I say you are condemned by your very silence."

"Just a minute," said the Marquis, his eyes large and guileless. "There is something I do not quite understand."

Idiot, thought Serafin, with a flash of anger. Why prolong this? I cannot bear . . . I cannot bear . . .

Balze, too, seemed annoyed. But he bowed politely. "Yes, Marquis?"

"Why did Serafin do all these things?"

"Why?" Balze stared at him. *"Why?* Does there have to be a why? It is because it is in this creature's nature, nothing more."

"I see," said the Marquis, nodding. "Is that why you have helped us? Because you are one of those free princes, are you not?"

"Yes," said Balze, impatiently. "I am the Bright One, the Leader, the Prince of the World."

"It seems to me," said the Marquis, "and forgive me if I am wrong, but you could do anything you want to. You could be the King of France, even."

"Yes." Balze rapped out the word.

"Then why aren't you?"

This time Balze could not stop the annoyance from filling his voice. "Because I have no time for such stupidities."

"The King of France is stupid?"

"Of course! All human things are stupid! All are dust: meaningless, worthless!" The voice was deathly cold. "They are but puppets whose strings I pull."

"I see," said the Marquis, very quietly. Everyone was staring at him now. He said then, "So that is *your* nature, Monsieur Balze. And that is why you must destroy Serafin and destroy us. Because we are *stupid*."

Serafin looked at him as if she had never seen him before. Something strange was happening inside her, and she had no words to put to it.

"You see, Monsieur Balze," continued the Marquis, "I have known Serafin since we were children. I know who she is. Yes, *she*. I do not understand her, I would not have lived the life she has, but I cannot believe what you say for I have *seen* with my own eyes. It is possible she has a divided nature, as you say. I have seen she has powers with my own eyes. I have been disquieted by them, for she is not exactly like the rest of us. Yet I cannot believe the rest. And my heart tells me she is not as you say, not because I am clever or know much at all, but because my blood and my flesh tell me so. We may be dust, Monsieur Balze, but I would rather be dust than a prince of the air without a soul. I would rather be dust than an empty darkness, a hungry abyss. At least dust mixed with water becomes dirt, and dirt grows crops and sustains life."

He turned away from them and quietly toward Serafin. "Forgive me for even allowing him to speak, for even allowing the lies to fall on the air."

Balze roared: "Lies! He can talk of lies! He, the *Marquis of Carabas*! Ah! That is like saying, *indeed*, the Duke of the Dirt!" And speaking savagely, he told them all the story of Frederic the miller's son and his only inheritance.

When he had finished, the ogre said, "So—not only traitor but impostor as well!" But he was interrupted in whatever it was he was going to say by Monsieur, who suddenly burst out laughing.

All eyes turned to him as he laughed and laughed and laughed. His eyes watered, his sides ached, and still he kept laughing. When at last he calmed down, he said, "Sorry, sorry, Balze! But you really do not expect me to believe that! Really, there is a limit to what one can believe!" As he laughed, his head seemed to clear, his heart to lift. He kept laughing, and thumping his thigh.

Balze watched him for a moment, his eyes cold as ice. Then he said, "Regardless of fools, justice must be done. If this . . . Marquis does not admit his servant is at fault, it follows they must both be guilty. They must be put to death, and immediately."

Elisabeth cried out, "No, oh no! If you do that, kill me too!"

"Gladly, my dear." Balze grinned at her. "It will not be a great loss."

Monsieur stopped laughing. Hiccuping, he said, his eyes fixed on Balze: "Come, come, Balze. A joke's a joke, but this is not funny. The King of France is coming here in a few days' time and we are not ready. Let us forget all this foolishness. I will certainly do my best to forget all the ridiculous things I have heard today. Let us ring for some soothing beverage and . . ."

Balze lifted a hand, and Monsieur fell to the ground, apparently stunned or even dead. "Now then," said Balze, as he advanced toward Serafin, "too long have I waited, and now I will not . . ."

"Balze." Turning in astonishment, he saw that the ogre was standing in the middle of the room, tottering, his face crumbling. "*Balze*. What have you done to my brother?"

Balze snorted. His eyes took on a red glow. "Your *brother*," he said contemptuously. "Fine words, my *Lord*. There is no space for "brother" left in that withered thing you call a soul. That pitiful thing you gave to me so easily."

"You have not answered my question, Balze." The ogre still stood, though his knees were shaking. He looked more like a ruined building now than a human being.

"Your brother is nothing," Balze said. He glared at the ogre. "As are you."

The ogre said nothing. Slowly, like a wall crumbling, he fell to his knees beside Monsieur. One hand reached stiffly out. "Balze. He has done nothing. I beg you."

"*Beg* now, is it? Instead of demand, demand, demand for years on years on years? Do this, do that, do the other, forgetting who is the servant, who is the master! Well, my *Lord,* your time has come and gone. You have lost everything: your power, your riches, your soul, your humanity. You are a shell now, a husk. Soon there will be a new Lord of Tenebran. Oh, not this fool, this false Marquis. But at Court, there are those who are more ready to listen."

"Balze. You forget." The ogre's voice was faint now, and seemed to come from very far away. "I have one thing left. My life."

"Your *life!* That means less than a grain of the soil these fools are so fond of."

"Nothing, perhaps, unless I *freely* give it. Because freedom is what I forfeited to you, but life is what you were bargaining with me. And if I give my life freely, without coercion, without treachery, then you are bound to take it. And you can take no other, for the bargain was with *me.*"

"You are unable to give freely." For the first time, there was a kind of panic in Balze's voice.

The ogre lifted his ruined head. His eyes suddenly cleared and, just for a moment, they all saw the direct green of his gaze. He spoke, and his voice was suddenly very loud and clear, its ringing tones filling the room. "I give you pity too, for you are truly pitiful, Prince of the World. There is no freedom, no real freedom in you, for you are *nothing* without us. And without my consent in the evil you command, you must vanish, for you and

135

your evil are *nothing* unless we choose you." There was a terrifying crash, like a bolt of lightning striking the earth, and in front of their eyes the ogre fell, like a stricken tree. Instantly, his body started collapsing in on itself, its color changing almost at once from pink to an awful gray, his limbs folding like dead branches rather than things of flesh and blood. But his eyes stayed open, fixed on Balze until the last moment, when they closed, never to open again.

At almost the same time, several things happened. Monsieur started up, Elisabeth and the Marquis, who had been as if frozen, rushed to the ogre, and Balze gave a great shriek and vanished, as completely as snow after rain. Serafin began to weep, the tears flowing from her eyes, down her cheeks and into her heart, into every corner of her. They were thawing and painful, joyful and sorrowful, tears such as she had never cried in her whole life. And she knew as the tears fell that her destiny had indeed come, and that now she was free. Not the false freedom of Balze and his kind, but one that willingly gave of itself, and that saw that truth came in the knowledge of the most humble, in the knowledge of flesh and blood.

Balze indeed was to be pitied, for never, in all eternity, would he have that knowledge—and that was a binding more terrible than any Law. He was indeed nothing without the choice of evil, and powerless in the face of love and loyalty.

» Epilogue «

The ogre was buried with all ceremony and respect, and Monsieur cried real tears of love, for he was a kindly man who never thought ill of anyone for very long. With the ogre dead and Balze gone, the castle became both less splendid and more real: no more a place of enchantment, but no longer a haunt of nightmare either. There were no more cracks in the walls, and there was an air of lightness in the rooms, but the gardens were smaller—they had to be, for the villages outside the castle grounds were large and prosperous. Monsieur had a portrait of his brother painted in oils, in the likeness of his youth, and everyone agreed that he had fine, if sorrowful, green eyes. Monsieur also relinquished the land granted by Serafin to the peasants of Tenebran, and far from causing him grief, this decision brought him a great lightness of heart.

The King came for his visit but only stayed a couple of hours. He had thought Tenebran to be much more splendid, and finding that it was merely a fine gentleman's house, and no rival to his own, was both relieved and disappointed. Ever afterward, the King thought of Tenebran and its inhabitants with a benign kind of indifference, which was lucky, really, for all of them. As to the box, he had given it to one of his courtiers, who had put it among his effects but never opened it in his life. It was, however, found many years later, broken and worn, after a great fire.

During his visit the King endowed the Marquis with an extra title and a castle only a short distance from Tenebran. This was rather a good thing, as the Marquis visited frequently during his courtship of Elisabeth.

Those two married in a wedding as beautiful as it was simple, and had many children. A couple of years after his daughter's wedding, Monsieur was married too, to a lady who read stories with him every day and who values his kind nature above anything else.

Balze was never seen again, at least not in that place. But no one made the mistake of thinking he was gone forever, for Balze and his kind flourish wherever the seed of hate grows in the darkness of the human heart. And his claim to being the Prince of the World was not an empty one—evil is a mystery as deep as it is real.

And what of Serafin, of Catou? She kept the name *Serafin*, for it reminded her not only of who her people had been long ago but also of who she had become. She is still to be seen sometimes at Carabas—as the young couple's estate is now called—sometimes in her human shape, occasionally in cat guise, but always treated with great honor and love. She returned, too, to that town far away where she first met another of her kind, the other half-angel, and she thinks that one day she may stay there. For she knows herself now, and she knows that the greatest of all destinies is to have the qualities of mercy and of love, the knowledge that is given to each of us if we open our heart. It is not a destiny that makes her sad or solemn anymore; along with tears, Serafin has discovered laughter, and laughter is what you hear most often in the places where she goes.

» Afterword «

This story is based, of course, on the story of *Puss in Boots*—the original seventeenth-century French version by Charles Perrault, which I first knew as a child under the name of *Le Chat Botté*.

Other influences have been the old stories of *matagots*, the cat-magicians in French legend who were supposed to make their lucky owners wealthy (and who were said to wear red boots, symbolizing the sunrise), and stories of the Court of Louis XIV, the original Sun King, who ruled France in the seventeenth and early eighteenth centuries. But this is not the "real" France of Louis XIV; rather, it is a fantasy one. The way the book opens is based on a real story from that time of a sixteen-year-old boy who saved a twenty-six-year-old woman, Francouneto, from being lynched by a mob as a witch. He was exiled from the village, with her, for his troubles.

And the story of the half-angel/half-human beings comes from a short passage in the Bible—in Genesis 6:4, if you want to look it up—that tells of how the "sons of God" (angels) came to Earth and took human wives, whose children were "the mighty men of renown of old." I have simply expanded on that and other stories of angels, as well as that of the Prince of the Angels, the Bright One, Lucifer himself. (It is also interesting to note in this context that the word *ogre* comes from *Orcus*, one of the names of Pluto, the god of the underworld.)

The name *Balze*, by the way, is a play on the biblical name Beelzebub, which is one of Lucifer's names (as is the Devil, and the Lord of the Flies).

» About the Author «

Sophie Masson was born in Indonesia of French parents, the third in a family of seven children. Her family came to Australia in 1963, and Sophie grew up in Sydney. She now lives in New South Wales, Australia, in a mud-brick house with her husband and three children. Sophie is a full-time writer and author.

Sophie Masson writes about herself:
My family is Catholic; my mother is particularly interested in the moral and ethical aspects of religion, my father in its mystical and symbolic aspects. Ours is also a rather lively, argumentative, and imaginative family, and we were exposed to a lot of different religious experiences. Having lived in Africa and Indonesia, I have always been interested in religion and the spiritual, and from a very early age, I felt what I call the "silent singing of the universe," which are other words for grace. I feel very strongly the idea that we are all of one flesh, one blood, and that what we do to others, we do to ourselves.

Contact us for more information about StarMaker Books by e-mail at *starmakerbooks@smp.org* or on our web site at *http://www.smp.org*. E-mail your reactions to Sophie Masson at *smasson@northnet.com.au,* or visit her web site at *http://members.xoom.com/sophiecastel/default.htm.*

ST★R*Maker* BOOKS

StarMaker Books are about young people like you who are struggling to become hopeful, healthy adults. These young people are special and unique characters. But you will see right away that they are not perfect people. Being unique does not mean being perfect. It means discovering your unique set of God-given gifts and growing them.

Be Your Own Star!

Find out more about your unique gifts by using this visualization: Start by writing your name in the middle of the dotted area below. React to each of the five personal traits listed on the opposite page by drawing a star-point outward to reflect your thoughts. Your star-points can be wide or narrow, short or long. Label each of the five points. When you are finished, you will see your own uniqueness shining back at you.

1. **Physical:** Do you feel good about yourself physically? Draw a point to reflect your sense of how physically gifted you are.

2. **Social:** Are your relationships honest and growing? Do you have the support you need to adjust to changes within your family and friendships?

3. **Emotional:** In your mind are you an emotionally balanced person? Can you express your strong feelings like anger and fear in healthful ways? Do you know when to let go of them?

4. **Spiritual:** Do you possess a "great soul"? Do you have a sense of the spiritual, mysterious dimensions of life? Where is God in your life?

5. **Intellectual:** Do you consider yourself a wise person? Can you state your views without being judgmental of others? Do you have the gift of seeing meanings below the surface issues?

Shine On!

- Once you have drawn your starter star, the sky's the limit. Draw another star a month from now. You will find that your uniqueness and God-given gifts change over time. Color your star to say more about yourself. Make a three-dimensional star out of foil or paper. Keep it in a folder or frame so you can refer to it again.